Flight

Flight

ELIZABETH
STOW ELLISON

Holiday House / *New York*

Library of Congress Cataloging-in-Publication Data
Ellison, Elizabeth Stow, 1970-
Flight / by Elizabeth Stow Ellison.
p. cm.
Summary: Twelve-year-old Samantha struggles with how
to best help her artistic older brother and parents
who will not have him tested for a learning disability.
ISBN 978-0-8234-2128-2 (hardcover)
[1. Brothers and sisters—Fiction. 2. Learning disabilities—Fiction.
3. Literacy—Fiction. 4. Family problems—Fiction.] I. Title.
PZ7.E476445Fl 2008
[Fic]—dc22
2008009372

Dedicated to my brother,
Jim,
a man who overcame
his disabilities
to take his own flight
in life.

Acknowledgments

My flight in becoming an author was not taken alone. I have many people to thank for helping me soar. First of all, I would like to thank my mom. Without her constant support and encouragement, I never would have been able to venture out of the nest. Steven Chudney, my wonderful agent, helped me sharpen my wings and prepare myself for the publishing world. I am so grateful to him for reaching out and taking a chance on me. Landing at Holiday House was my greatest fortune, and Julie Amper made the entire process of turning a manuscript into a novel a joyful breeze. Her enthusiasm gave me the lift I needed to see my way through the revisions. I am grateful for my teachers who taught me how to read and how to believe in myself. I am so fortunate to have friends who listened to and believed in my dreams about becoming an author. I am going to enjoy every moment of my flight, and it is my hope that you, the reader, will soar as you, too, take flight.

Flight

Chapter 1

"I dare you." Evan, Gilbert, and I stood at the chain-link fence that wrapped around Hank's Apple Orchard.

"No way!" Gilbert said.

"It's simple. Hop over the fence, climb the nearest tree, pick three apples, and run back. You'd go, huh, Samantha?"

I nodded, even though just the thought of doing such a thing scared me to death.

"It says right there," said Gilbert, pointing to a sign, "'Trespassers will be prosecuted.'"

Evan just grinned and squinted up at the sunny sky with his hands on his hips.

"You're stalling, Bert," Evan accused. Gilbert hated it when Evan called him Bert.

"If it's so simple, you go," he said, jutting out his chin and trying his best to look tough.

That was all Evan needed. He was up and over the fence in a flash. But he didn't run, and he didn't climb the nearest tree. We watched him stroll along until he disappeared into the middle of the orchard. I think I even heard him whistle a tune.

"He'll get caught. We'll all get caught!" Gilbert squeezed his eyes shut and shook his head. No more tough guy.

"Don't be such a worrywart," I said, my stomach churning.

"Hank's got a gun, you know. Says he's sick of getting ripped off."

"Three apples isn't a rip-off."

The two of us laced our fingers in the links of the fence and peered into the orchard. The afternoon sun was hot, though a breeze offered some relief as it ruffled the leaves of the trees. The breeze carried the sweet, rotten scent of the apples on the ground, skins puckered, full of holes from worms, ants, and other bugs.

Flies buzzed, and birds darted in and out of the thick foliage. A dog suddenly started barking frantically.

"That's it! I knew it! I told you! Let's get out of

here!" Gilbert backed away from the fence, looking in all directions. He started gasping for air, and his face turned as red as the apples that hung on the trees.

"Gil, come on. Don't have an asthma attack now. It's not a big deal. You always make such a big deal of . . ."

A loud cracking sound startled us. The single gunshot set the dog barking even more frantically and sent birds flapping out of the trees. Now I was the one gasping for air.

I started clawing at the fence, trying to climb over, but Gilbert was holding me back, weighing me down.

I caught a glimpse of a moving figure out of the corner of my eye. Then the sound of pounding feet grew louder, and there came Evan, running full speed with a wild look on his face. He clambered over the fence and raced off, laughing.

With a quick check to see if he was being followed, the two of us gave chase. We ran across an empty field into a thicket of pines.

"Here you go." Evan handed each of us a perfect red apple. I took mine with a shaky hand and looked up at my brother, who was smiling from ear to ear. He wasn't even winded.

"What happened?"

"What do you mean?"

"We heard a gunshot!" I yelled.

"No way. You must have heard a car backfire."

"I know what I heard," I said.

"Where did you go, anyway?" Gilbert asked.

"All the way to the other side and then around the whole orchard," Evan said, taking a big bite of his apple.

"Why?"

"For kicks." Juice dribbled down his chin, and he wiped it off with the back of his hand.

Furious, I threw my apple at Evan, and it grazed his shoulder. He flinched and looked at me in shock. Then he laughed, which made me even angrier.

He was always doing things for kicks, moving from one stunt to another until he got caught. Then he'd lie low for a while and let our parents' or whoever's tempers settle.

Here I was again, wondering why Evan was always risking getting into trouble—or worse. The sound of the gunshot still rang in my ears as I looked up at his smiling eyes.

"Sammy." He struggled to suppress his laughter. "I told you. It was a car or a firecracker. Hank didn't even see me."

I shrugged. "Well . . . maybe . . ."

Evan grinned. Then he looked at Gilbert. "Okay, man. Your turn. Go get three more."

"No way! That was too close," Gilbert said. He turned and trotted away, his uneaten apple cupped in his hand. Evan laughed, pitched his core, and wiped his hands on his shirt.

As we trudged back past the orchard, I felt like it loomed larger than before and the sweet smell had soured. I looked up at Evan, whose eyes were fixed on the orchard. He glanced at me. "It was a backfire," he said. Then, after a moment, "It was." I wondered who he was trying to convince.

Chapter 2

Our blue house sat at the top of a long gravel drive-way lined with tall pine trees. From the bottom of the driveway, we could see the peak of the roof and the chimney. We heard the familiar pound of the basket-ball against the backboard and hoop our father had mounted on the garage.

Our older brother, Andy, was practicing free throws. Sweat poured down his face and made his dark blond hair look more like it was brown. He was so focused on making his next shot, he didn't notice us.

"Think fast!" Evan shouted, and whisked the ball right out of his hands.

"Knock it off!" Andy yelled. Evan just laughed and ran circles around him. Evan was going in for a slam dunk when Andy grabbed him by the back of his shirt collar. Evan made a kind of choking noise, and the ball went bouncing into the hedges.

"You don't have to be such a bully. I would've given you the ball," he said, straightening out his shirt.

Evan was actually a much better ball player than Andy was. The coach of the varsity team had asked him to join even though he was only a freshman, but Evan had turned him down, saying that he wasn't the competitive type. The truth was that if the coach had taken a look at Evan's grades, he wouldn't have bothered to ask. A "D" average disqualified him from all sports whether he was the competitive type or not.

Andy practiced night and day, setting his hopes on earning a scholarship to college next fall. At six feet four inches, he had the height, and the trophies on the shelves in his room proved he had the talent.

When the school year started, Dad kept saying, "This is your year, son." He'd clap Andy on the back, and this look would come over his face like he wished it was his senior year again, his year to be a jock and a superstar.

"Isn't it exciting?" Mom gushed. "Any ideas about who you'll take to Homecoming or Prom?" Andy laughed this off, but Mom was serious. I was pretty sure she had my first prom dress picked out, and it was a good six years off.

"The Class of '83," Andy said, a mix of excitement and disbelief in his voice. Grandma and Grandpa Sheffield had already booked their flight from Florida for the big graduation day in June.

I guess it was pretty exciting.

I left my brothers in a heated game of one on one and went looking for Mom.

"In here, honey!"

I dropped my book bag and headed to the kitchen, where she was standing at the sink, holding a spoon and the last of a chocolate cream pie.

"You're not . . ." I started to ask, but she answered me by leaning over the sink and spitting out a mouthful of pie filling.

"I hate it when you do that," I complained, but she didn't hear me over the spray of the water and the hum of the disposal. Then she scraped a final huge bite from the pie plate, shoved it into her mouth, and chewed with her eyes closed like she was in heaven. Again, she spat and rinsed.

"Yuck."

"Honey." She smiled with chocolaty teeth. "When you get to be my age, you can't just eat whatever you want. This way I get some of the flavor without all of the calories."

Weren't the workout videos enough? I wondered. She came over to me and put her hands on my shoulders.

"How was your day?"

"Fine." I could smell the chocolate on her breath.

A frown came into her eyes. "What have you been up to?"

"Nothing. Just playing." The image of us running from the orchard flashed in my mind.

"You look like you've been running wild, and you smell sweaty. A girl your age needs to . . ."

I hated the way my beautiful mom could make me feel ugly with just a few words. She looked beyond me out the kitchen window. We could hear the scuff of sneakers and the bounce of the ball. A smile flickered on her face before she strode out to the porch.

"Evan, come do your homework."

The game continued.

"Let's go, Evan James!"

Evan made a basket, declared himself the winner, and jogged up the front steps.

"We weren't finished!" Andy called after him, making what he counted as a three-pointer. He went back to free throws while Evan lugged his backpack to the kitchen table.

"You too, Samantha," Mom said. She watched us for a moment. I got started on my spelling homework while Evan pawed through his backpack. Eventually he pulled out a folder, and Mom was satisfied. She patted Evan on the back and then tried to get his hair to go the way she thought it should.

"Mo-om." Evan groaned, ducking away.

"Okay." She pulled her hands away and looked at the clock on the oven. "I've got to get going. I have a PTA meeting at the high school. Dinner's in the fridge. You kids can eat whenever you want. Daddy's working late tonight." Her voice trailed off as she ran upstairs to freshen up. Mom was on nearly every committee our town of Orinda had to offer, which was good, because she sure did have a lot to say about things.

When she came back down, the chocolate smell had been replaced by mint from a quick swipe of the toothbrush. I watched her reapply her dark red lipstick using a little mirror from her purse.

"Hey, Mom, can you help me with this?" Evan held up a worksheet from the folder he'd retrieved earlier. Mom stopped, looked at him, and then glanced at the clock again.

"Ask your father when he gets home. Or maybe Andy can help you." And then she was out the door.

Evan watched her car pull away, and as soon as the taillights of her brown station wagon (Mom called it gold) disappeared, he stuffed his folder back into his book bag, gave me a wink, and went out to continue his game with Andy.

I walked over to the sink and was grossed out by a chocolate smudge Mom had missed.

"I don't think I'll ever eat chocolate cream pie again," I said to myself as I pulled two sugar cookies out of the cookie jar. Then I decided to give makeup another try.

I went to my room, grabbed my *Young Teen* magazine, and pulled my little yellow makeup kit out from behind my dollhouse. My grandparents had given me the dollhouse for my fifth birthday. It came with a mom, a dad, two sons, and a daughter. I used to play with it for hours, but the dollhouse was dusty now, and I could see strings of spiderweb running from room to room.

In the bathroom I set my cookies aside and sat cross-legged on the counter so I could be closer to the mirror. I opened my magazine to the dog-eared page of "Maggie's Makeup Tips" and studied the directions.

"Blue eyeliner goes on first." I picked up the thin blue pencil, pulled down my lower lid, and carefully drew a line along the tender pink skin. This made my eye water, but I ignored it. Line drawn, I blinked and inspected my work. Like so many times before, I wasn't happy, but I moved on to Step Two anyway.

"Apply dark blue eye shadow to the upper lid." I did this and then used the lighter blue shadow to "blend" as Step Three instructed. And finally, mascara. I brushed the pasty black goo onto my lashes. It clumped, and my bottom lashes stuck together. I tried to pick them apart, and in doing so, I poked my eye and dropped the brush.

"Ugh!" I groaned, and squeezed my eye shut. I fished the brush out of the sink, smearing mascara along the way, and got down from the counter to peer at myself in the mirror. I definitely looked nothing like Maggie—more like a freckled prizefighter who had just lost another match.

"I am ugly." I sighed and looked at the tips again.

Makeup was a sore subject in our house. For my twelfth birthday, my friend Gabby had given me a little makeup set. It came with lip gloss, blush, mascara, and an array of blue eye shadows. Before dinner one evening, I had experimented with it, and my grand entrance was met by roars of laughter from Andy, even a laugh from Evan, and surprising anger from Daddy, who declared that no daughter of his would wear makeup until she was in high school!

"That's three years away!" Mom and I had cried in unison, but Daddy was not swayed, and by the time I'd finished washing my face, my chicken and mashed potatoes were cold.

"There's my pretty girl," Daddy had said. I steeled myself against his compliment and dug into my potatoes.

Later that night when Mom came to tuck me in, she promised to work on Daddy. "He just doesn't understand us girls sometimes."

I picked up the soap, washed away another failed attempt, stored my makeup kit and magazine, and headed out to watch my brothers play basketball.

The October sun set, forcing the end of the game. From the look on Andy's red face, I figured Evan was the winner. I followed them inside, and without a word Andy dashed upstairs to get to the shower first.

"He's such a sore loser," Evan said, leaning over the sink to drink from the faucet. He ran his head under the stream of water before shutting it off.

"Let's see what's for dinner," he said, opening

the fridge and ignoring the drops of water dotting his shirt.

I watched him pull a glass dish from the fridge. He lifted the lid, sniffed, and waved me over.

"What do you think?" he asked.

I looked at the mix of vegetables, breadcrumbs, and creamy stuff. "I think we need to get Andy to take us out for burgers."

He laughed. "Good idea."

Andy was just as happy with this idea, and the three of us piled into his El Camino and headed for Nation Burgers and Ice Cream, the only burger place in town. Orinda was too small for a McDonald's. Evan's hair had air-dried by the time we arrived.

The place was busy with tables and booths full of high-school students, many of them Andy's friends.

"Here," Andy handed Evan a ten-dollar bill and left us to order while he joined a group of friends in the corner booth.

"Welcome to Nation Burgers and Ice Cream. How can I help you?" asked a pimply kid in a monotone voice.

"Two Value Meals and a Kid's Meal," Evan said.

"I'll have a Value Meal instead of a Kid's Meal," I said.

Evan looked at me.

"I'm almost thirteen, you know."

"You just turned twelve."

"So," Pimple interrupted, "Three Value Meals and a Kid's Meal. That'll be eleven ninety-four."

"No Kid's Meal," Evan and I said. Pimple's shoulders fell and his face reddened as he tried to figure out how to take the extra charge off the register. He punched some keys, and each time the register beeped an angry response until he pushed something and got one long, nonstop beep.

"Uh . . . Bob?" he waved to the manager, who wasn't much older than he was. The manager rolled his eyes, walked over, and moved Pimple out of the way. With the turn of a key and the press of a button, the mistake was erased. The manager gave Pimple a "get it right next time" look and then marched back to the kitchen.

"Will that be all?" Pimple asked.

Evan nodded, and suddenly I felt sorry for Pimple. When he reached for the money from Evan, he gazed at the group in the corner booth. They were all smiles and no pimples.

"Fifty-six cents is your change. Here's your number." He handed me a green flag on a stick. On the flag, the number "17" was painted in orange, and at our table there was a little rack for us to post it.

"Let's play Pac-Man," Evan suggested. He held the top three records on the Pac-Man machine at Nation Burger. Before he dropped his quarter in the slot, we checked the screen, and sure enough the top three spots read, "EJS." Evan let the quarter go, and I pushed start.

He got to the Peach Level quickly before he lost two men. Then big Freddy Hicks came over, put his quarter on the machine, and declared, "I'm next."

"Get ready to wait a long time. He's the best." I said. Freddy smirked and looked on as Evan sped Pac-Man through the complicated maze.

He was just about to beat one of his records when Freddy shoved Evan, and the ghosts devoured his last Pac-Man.

"What the hell?" Evan yelled loud enough to attract the attention of Andy and the same manager who had helped us before. Evan faced Freddy, and thinking they were going to get into a fight, I grabbed Evan's hand.

"What's the problem?" the manager demanded.

Evan glared angrily, but Freddy just shrugged. "I don't have a problem. Do you have a problem?" he said. Evan looked at the floor and kept his mouth shut. He pulled his hand from my grasp.

"He . . ." I started to explain, but Evan stopped me.

"Keep it under control or leave," the manager warned. Andy stood behind the manager, shaking his head.

"What was that all about?" Andy asked.

"Nothing," Evan said, quickly sitting down and unwrapping his burger.

"Stupid Freddy Hicks pushed Evan and made him lose when he was almost going to beat his best record ever," I said, taking a seat.

Andy glanced over at the game, where Freddy was playing away.

"He's just a dumb bully. Don't let him get to you."

"It's not fair," I said, looking at Andy, who poured a pool of ketchup on his tray for his fries. Evan did the same, and the two gobbled their food.

"Yo, Sheffield!" We looked toward the booth in the corner, where a group of Andy's friends were sliding over to make room for him. He gathered up his tray and joined them.

"Hey! Hello there, Evan and Samantha!" Mr. and Mrs. O'Connor, wearing matching green Izod sweaters, were heading our way. They were friends of our parents. "How sweet," Mrs. O'Connor said. "The two of you having dinner together. I wish our kids got along as well as you two. Your parents must be so proud."

"They've done a fine job. A fine job. Hey! We hear your brother is doing quite well on the team this year and that he's in the running for valedictorian. I'm sure he'll have to beat the colleges away with a stick," Mr. O'Connor said. Evan and I just looked at him. He smiled way too much.

"Andy's over there if you want to talk to him about it," I said, pointing toward the booth, but Mr. O'Connor didn't take the hint.

"Hey, how about you, Evan? Taking up any sports? Going to follow in your brother's footsteps, now that you've started high school?"

"Nope," Evan said quickly. Mrs. O'Connor's huge smile faded a bit, while Mr. O'Connor was undaunted. "Well, there's time yet. I'm sure you'll find something that interests you."

Evan didn't make an effort to agree, and there was an awkward moment. Then Mr. O'Connor said, "Hey, we'll let you get back to your dinner. We'll see you at the game on Friday."

Evan looked after them and scoffed.

"He sure says 'hey' a lot," I said. Evan laughed

at this and helped himself to my fries. I glanced over at the Pac-Man game. Freddy Hicks was already out of quarters. I bet he didn't even break the Top Ten.

At home Evan went to his room, and soon the familiar sound of the Beastie Boys blared from behind his closed door. He was probably working on another sketch, taking advantage of the fact that no one was home to get on his case about studying. He was an incredible artist. He'd always do pictures for me of Snoopy, Kermit, Miss Piggy; you name it, he'd draw it. He had his own ideas too, and I was amazed at how with just a few strokes he made the character come to life. I wished our parents were as impressed. They recognized his talent but said that if he put as much effort into school as he did into his drawings, he'd do better academically. Then, as Dad put it, he could enjoy such "frivolous activities."

Andy went to his room to get started on his homework, and I settled in front of the TV. Not long after, Daddy came home.

"Hi, Baby." He smiled and kissed me on the head. "Did Mom leave dinner?"

"Yes."

"Oh, good," he said, loosening his tie and opening

the fridge. He leaned on the door with one arm and reached in with the other. I heard the clink of the glass lid, but he left it where it was and poured himself a bowl of cereal. To go with it, he heated a cup of coffee from the pot that had started the day. He sat at the table and ate slowly.

Andy came down for a soda and joined Daddy at the table.

"It looks like we're going to have a good season. Coach said we have a shot at the CIF Championship."

"Season hasn't even started yet."

"Yeah, but coach says it's looking good."

Daddy nodded and ate the rest of his cereal. He looked up at Evan's door, and I wondered if this would be a fight night or not. It used to be that when Dad got home from work, he would ask Evan about his homework, and the discussion would quickly become a fight.

"Have you done your homework?"

"Yeah."

"Show it to me."

"I said I did it."

"I said show it to me."

And if Evan had anything to show, Daddy would look it over and launch into a tirade about how a first grader could do better. Then Evan would say something rude and get sent to his room for the night.

Daddy looked like he was contemplating his choices. Get into it with Evan or leave him be. To my relief he chose to leave him be, and he and Andy talked basketball some more.

"Scouts from UCLA are coming on Friday, even though it's a pre-season game," Andy said.

"Are you interested in UCLA?"

"Maybe. I met one of their scouts last year. He seemed interested."

"Of course he was interested in you." Dad poured himself a second bowl of cereal. "Is coach putting you in the starting lineup on Friday?"

"Yeah."

"That's my boy." The deep murmur of their voices was comforting.

I was sent to bed long before Mom got home. That wasn't unusual, since she and the other moms usually went out after their meetings. The thing with me was that I had a hard time sleeping—always have. Even the slightest noise wakes me. So, when Mom closed her car door later that night, I woke. I listened to her shoes crunch in the gravel and then clomp up the steps and into the house. I even heard her hushed voice as she greeted Daddy. The two talked in the family room for a while, and then upstairs in their room.

"So, no one ate my casserole?"

"Honey, I'll take some for lunch tomorrow."

"And the next day and the next day," Mom said. The two laughed, and I drifted off to sleep.

I woke in the middle of the night to go to the bathroom. On my way back I glanced into Evan's room. It took a few seconds for what I'd seen to actually register. His bed was empty, his pajamas were in a pile on the floor, and his window was wide open. What was he up to? I leaned out his window, but I saw no sign of him anywhere.

I paced nervously in front of his window, stopping every once in a while to peer out into the black night. There was no moon, and the Indian summer air was unusually warm and sweet. I was about to go tell Mom and Daddy that Evan had disappeared when he came walking into his room. We scared the heck out of each other. When we got over our fright, I whispered, "Where were you?"

"I went to see the owls," he said with a shrug.

"Owls?" I shouted. Evan froze and looked toward the hall with wide eyes. But our parents had not woken. Evan slid his window closed and picked up his pajamas.

"Are you sleepwalking?" I asked, pinching his arm.

"Stop it," he said, brushing my hand away, half

laughing, half irritated. "Go back to bed." I knew that I wasn't going to get more of an explanation.

For the rest of that night, my dreams were filled with owls, like the one that was always trying to count how many licks it took to get to the center of a Tootsie Pop but never made it because he couldn't resist the urge to chomp.

Chapter 3

Friday morning came with the usual rush.

"At least it's Friday," Evan said when I passed him in the hall on the way back from taking a shower. In my room, I worked on figuring out what to wear. I was on my fifth outfit when Mom called me for the second time.

"Samantha Leigh! Breakfast is on the table!"

I looked in the mirror on my closet door. At my feet were piles of rejected outfits. Things were either too big or too small, or the colors just didn't seem right. I was on my way into my closet for a sixth time when Mom yelled again. This time her voice cracked angrily. I groaned and stomped downstairs.

"For goodness' sake, Samantha!" Mom scolded when I stepped into the kitchen.

"I was just . . ." I started to explain, but Mom's angry face and Dad's look of irritation as he glanced up from his newspaper made my eyes well up with tears. Dad put his paper down and sighed loudly. Andy and Evan, who had been eating their cereal, stopped and looked at me.

"Uh . . . what's the drama queen crying about now?" Andy asked.

"Shut up!" I yelled.

"That's enough!" Daddy boomed. "Samantha, what is it?"

I wiped my eyes with the back of my hand.

"Nothing." Everyone groaned, and I sat down to a bowl of soggy cereal.

I really don't know why I was crying. Tears just seemed to come a lot easier lately. "I don't have anything to wear," I said finally.

"You better not touch my socks again," Andy warned with a glance under the table.

"Who wants your stinky socks anyway?" I muttered, blushing with embarrassment.

Back before school started, Mom had taken me clothes shopping. Inside Mervyn's I told Mom about how all the girls were wearing leg warmers. I wanted a pair of rainbow-striped leg warmers more than anything in the world.

"That's such a fad. You watch. In three weeks leg warmers will be out and something else will be all the rage." She grinned. Mom was the expert on everything, especially fashion, and her taste was starting to get in the way of what I wanted for myself. "Believe me," she continued, "I've been there. It's exhausting to try to keep up with the latest fashions, not to mention . . ." She plucked a bright yellow pair from the giant rack of leg warmers of every color and pattern and glanced at the price tag. "Expensive! Eighteen dollars for these?"

"I like them. Can't I get one pair? Please?" I held up the exact rainbow pair I wanted and quickly put my thumb over the twenty-dollar price. I guess stripes cost more.

"If you want a pair, save your allowance and we'll come back." This really made me angry, because we both knew that I was not good at saving money. I suffered through the rest of the shopping trip and got home with my usual mix-and-match pants and tops, a skirt I probably wouldn't wear, and a pack of underwear.

On my way to my room, I saw a pair of Andy's

tube socks lying on his bed. In a flash of brilliance, I grabbed his socks, sneaked Mom's scissors out of her sewing kit, then cut the feet off both socks. I put the socks on and pulled them up to just below my knees.

With great care I arranged them so they were bunched and bulky like real leg warmers with two blue stripes at the top. I stood in front of my mirror, delighted with how they looked. My plan was to carry them to school in my backpack and put them on once I got there.

I was taking one last look at my creation when Andy came barging in.

"Hey, Sam, Mom wants you—" He stopped abruptly when his eyes caught sight of my leg warmers, and I watched recognition slowly wash over his face.

"What did you do to my socks?"

"Nothing." It was worth a try, but Andy didn't buy it. He knocked me down and wrestled one of my homemade leg warmers off.

"You cut my socks!" He yelled, and stomped down the hall, screaming, "Mom! Mom!" just like a baby. "She cut my socks!"

Mom came rushing in. "I . . ." There was nothing I could say, and Mom was confused.

"She cut my socks!" Andy repeated, waiving the footless sock in the air.

Mom looked from the sock in Andy's hand to the one I still had on, and I watched her work really hard to keep from laughing.

"It's not funny!" Andy and I both cried.

Mom sighed. "No, it's not funny at all." Then she told me I could forget saving allowance for leg warmers because I'd have to buy Andy a new pair of socks.

"Great. That'll take two years," Andy muttered.

"Not if Mom and Dad increase my allowance," I suggested.

"Forget it," Mom snapped, and went back to cooking dinner. Andy demanded that I give him his other sock and angrily stomped off.

That was almost two months ago, and Andy still wasn't over it. It was just a dumb pair of socks.

"Interesting." Daddy said, and turned the newspaper toward Mom, pointing to a picture of some businessman. "IBM is going to give Xerox and Apple a run for their money. They're developing the technology to do something called 'windowing' or splitting the computer screen into several sections for different tasks."

"Hmm. You lost me, honey, with all that mumbo jumbo." She grinned and pushed the newspaper away.

Daddy chuckled and stuck the paper in the side pocket of his briefcase. He would read the rest of it on his BART ride to work in the city. Mom hopped up from the table, grabbed his sack lunch, and handed it to him with a kiss good-bye. Usually Daddy headed out the door then, but this morning he came over to my side of the table and patted me on the back.

"Bye, beautiful girl." He smiled and left. I felt a little better.

Mom cleared the table, telling the three of us to hurry up. Andy grabbed his books, and in a moment the engine of his car roared and he sped down the driveway.

"Mom?" Evan asked.

"What, honey? I'm in a hurry." A hint of a smile lit up Evan's eyes.

"Can you sign this? It's a permission slip for shop class, so we can use the power tools." He pulled the paper from his back pocket.

"You're supposed to have your father sign these things."

"I forgot. I need it today."

She looked around for a pen.

"Here." He held out a pen and flattened the

creased note on the table. Mom signed, kissed us good-bye, and dashed upstairs. Soon the shower was running. Evan returned the note to his pocket.

"That wasn't a note for shop class, was it?" I asked as I followed him to the door. He stopped in his tracks and turned to look at me.

"Naa. It's a note saying something about me not doing my homework in English."

"They'll find out. They always do."

Evan shrugged and glanced up at Mom and Dad's bedroom. "I'm not even in shop." He laughed an angry laugh and left me standing on the front porch.

How could Mom be so clueless? Even I knew Evan didn't take shop. I pulled the door closed and ran to catch up with Evan.

Chapter 4

On the way home from school, Gilbert and I debated whether or not our teacher, Mrs. Teedle, wore a wig. I didn't think so, but Gilbert was sure of it.

"Come on! Every time she scratches her head, all of her hair moves!"

I tried to picture it. Her curly brown hair moving in unison.

"You're wrong," I said as we reached his house. Gilbert's smile disappeared when he saw that his dad's car was parked in front of his house.

"This is your weekend to go to your dad's, huh?"

"Yeah. He's got a new girlfriend, so now we have to do everything she wants, like shopping and feeding the ducks at the lake and more shopping."

"Hi, Samantha." Gilbert's mom came outside

when she saw us. "Gilbert, honey, your dad's waiting. Let's go."

"Bye." Gilbert waved and followed his dad to his car. I couldn't imagine what it would be like to have to move back and forth between parents. I remember when they first split up and Gilbert said it was cool because he had two of everything. Gilbert was small for his age, but he looked especially small in his dad's brown-and-white VW van. I could just see his curly red hair and the top of his thick glasses as he looked up at his dad, who had the same curly hair and glasses.

At home I found Mom working in the garden.

"Hi, sweetie. Want to come help me pull weeds?"

"Sure." I set my backpack on the porch and joined her in the flower bed. The little weeds slipped out of the moist ground easily.

"So, how's Gilbert?" she asked as she mercilessly plucked a snail from under one of her mums and chucked it as far as she could.

"His parents are still divorced," I said, and looked to where I imagined the snail was writhing in pain, cracked shell and all.

Mom looked up from her weeding. "That isn't what I asked. Though, since you brought it up, I do think it's tragic."

I struggled with one of the larger weeds and decided not to tell her about his dad's new girlfriend. Whenever Mom asked about Gilbert, it was either to talk about why his parents were divorced or to bug me about why I spent so much time with him.

She always said, "You should be doing girl things with other girls. What about Gabby or Melissa? Kelly's a nice girl."

Gabby, Melissa, and Kelly were friends, and I did spend time with them, but I never understood why choosing to spend more time with Gilbert mattered. I didn't think of what he and I did as girl or boy things, just friend things, and I liked it that way.

One time Gilbert and I spent most of a Saturday trying out ways to get into the *Guinness Book of World Records*. We tried setting a record for standing on one foot the longest, but we only made it twenty minutes before Gilbert sneezed and lost his balance. Then we tried to set a record for the number of times we could catch popcorn in our mouths. We only got up to twelve catches in a row when his mom made us stop because we were making a mess. We considered trying to see if we could blow the world's biggest bubble, but we couldn't figure out how to measure it without getting gum all over the tape measure.

Even after a day of failed record-setting attempts,

Gilbert was not defeated. He suggested that I try to grow the longest hair in the world, and maybe, just maybe, he could break the record for the most freckles. He promised to count, and I said I'd give growing my hair out a try. That's what I liked about Gilbert.

"Be sure to get the roots," Mom said when the stem and leaves of an overgrown weed broke away in my hand. She nudged me aside and tried to get the rest of the weed.

"I just know that if Gilbert's mom put on a little makeup now and then and got a homemade meal on the table . . ." She worked her gloved fingers into the dirt in an effort to get to the roots.

"What?" I asked.

"Let's just say she'd probably still be married."

"Really?"

She nodded, then frowned at my weeding job.

"I don't think they got divorced because of makeup."

Mom winked at me like she does when she thinks I'm too young to really understand something and moved on to another section of the garden. I brushed off my hands and retreated to the tire swing to watch her work. Most of the times I tried to help her with something went like this. I ended up watching while she redid my work.

She wore red gloves that matched her sun hat and garden clogs, and she hummed to herself happily as she battled weeds and tossed more snails. Last spring her garden won First Place in the Orinda Neighbors' Garden Tour. The prize was a green trophy in the shape of a thumb.

"I think I'll plant some bulbs here, and . . ."

Just then the phone rang.

"Will you get that?"

I hopped off the swing and dashed inside.

"Hello?"

"This is Miss Porter, one of Evan's teachers. May I speak with Mr. or Mrs. Sheffield?"

"Uh . . ." I felt a nervous lump rise in my throat. "They're busy right now. Can I take a message?"

"Just let them know that I called. I'd appreciate it if they would give me a call at the school. I'll be here until about five o'clock, or they can reach me on Monday."

"Okay," I said, and hung up.

"Who was it?" Mom asked from the door as she kicked off her garden clogs.

"Wrong number." The words just fell out of my mouth.

"Oh." She set a basket of flowers on the table. Then she filled a vase with water and started arranging. I scooped a handful of fish crackers from the sack in the pantry.

"Don't spoil your dinner."

"I won't," I said, casually glancing out the kitchen window in hopes of catching Evan.

"You know, your room is a mess. No wonder you think you don't have anything to wear." Snip, snip with the clippers. She trimmed leaves and thorns, never looking up from her work.

I slipped outside to wait for Evan. I pulled my bicycle out of the garage and pedaled down to the end of the driveway. Then I rode back up, made a loop, and coasted back down. On my third loop I skidded to a stop right in front of Evan.

"Hey, you," he greeted, and started to move past me.

"Wait!" I called, looking back at the house to see if Mom had noticed us. There was no sign that she had. "Follow me," I said, leading him behind the garage. I parked my bike and swallowed nervously checking again for any signs of Mom.

"What's so serious?" Evan asked, trying to suppress a smile.

"Your teacher called."

"Mr. Edwards?"

"No. She said her name was Miss Porter."

"That's my science teacher. Is Mom pissed?"

"She doesn't know. I answered, and then I told Mom it was a wrong number." I whispered the last part of my explanation.

"Wow. Nice going, Sammy." He tousled my hair.

"No! Not nice going!" I brushed his hand away and stepped back.

"Relax. They won't find out what you did." He wasn't smiling now. "Look, thanks for helping me out. Things aren't going too good in school right now."

They never have, I said to myself.

The ring of the telephone made me jump in panic. We both stood still and strained to listen.

"Hello?" Mom answered.

We held our breath.

"Hi, Glenda!"

I closed my eyes and leaned against the garage in relief. Evan rubbed his face and ran his hands through his hair.

"What did you do, anyway?"

"It's not a big deal," he said quietly, eyes glued to the ground. He jammed his hands into his pockets and kicked the back step with his foot.

Just then, Mom surprised us both by coming outside with a bag of trash.

"What are you up to?"

"Nothing," I said quickly.

"The O'Connors will be here any minute."

"Why?" Evan asked.

Mom clicked her tongue. "It's Friday. We're going to your brother's basketball game."

"Do I have to go?" Evan asked. "It's a pre-season game. Doesn't even count."

"Don't start. Of course you're going. You might actually like school if you took an interest in what goes on there," she said. Evan rolled his eyes.

Back inside she grabbed her Orinda High School sweatshirt and pulled it over her head, careful not to mess up her hair. Pinned to the front of the sweatshirt was a big round button with a picture of Andy in his basketball uniform. The school colors were purple and green, and in the ultimate show of school spirit, Mom had laced purple and green shoelaces in her sneakers.

A honk out front signaled that the O'Connors

had arrived. Mom flung her purse over her shoulder, and we followed her out to the car and piled into the back seat. Mr. and Mrs. O'Connor were wearing matching school sweatshirts with buttons of their three daughters, who were cheerleaders. I just had to see if they were wearing matching shoelaces too. It took some doing, but I leaned forward and glanced over the front seat. They were wearing not only green and purple shoelaces but matching white canvas shoes and khaki pants as well.

I looked at Evan to see if he noticed the same thing, but he was staring out the window. Mom would call it pouting, and I braced myself for her to tell him to knock it off, which would make Evan pout even more. Fortunately, Mom and the O'Connors got to talking, and we were all spared an argument.

The school gym was packed. Cheerleaders jumped, clapped, and danced to the music of OHS's award-winning marching band. Hopes were high that this would be the band's year to go to the Rose Parade. The closest they'd been was the Hollywood Christmas Parade the Sunday after Thanksgiving last year. Posted on the wall behind the band section was a banner that read, "Rose Parade or Bust!"

It was the O'Connors' night to work in the snack shop, so they waved good-bye, promising to root for

Andy, and headed over to the booth that was set up in front of the gym.

As we found a seat in the bleachers, the school mascot, a panther, came bouncing out, and the crowd went wild. The guy in the panther suit did six back-flips in a row, landing in the locked arms of two other cheerleaders on the final flip.

"Wow! He's good," Mom said. "See what fun you can have if you get involved in your school?"

"You want me to be a cheerleader?" Evan asked.

"Not necessarily. But look at the band and the players, all the groups of friends."

"I've got friends," Evan said quickly.

Actually, he had one best friend named Brian, who had moved away at the beginning of the summer. His dad had gotten a job transfer, and they had moved all the way across the country to Maine. Mom and Dad said it was too expensive for them to talk on the phone and that they should write to each other. I guess Brian's parents thought phone calls were too expensive too, because he never called. He wrote once, but Evan didn't write back. It made him angry when I brought it up, so I didn't.

"What friends?" Mom asked. Evan winced.

"Don't start, Mom," he said, getting up.

"Oh, Evan, don't be so sensitive," Mom complained.

Without looking back, he made his way down the bleachers and outside. Mom looked after him and pursed her lips. Then she saw a fellow PTA member and waved, a renewed smile on her face.

"Honey, save these seats. I need to go talk with Mr. Jones."

From where I sat, I could see Andy and his team warming up on the court, Evan standing just outside the door, and Mom talking with a growing group of acquaintances. I watched high-school girls flit about, hugging their friends as if they hadn't seen each other in ages. They all wore leg warmers and tight Jordache jeans, and had perfect makeup and hairstyles. It seemed like there were three groups of girls to belong to: cute little ones with pigtails, freckles, and lollipop mouths; those older girls who were so sophisticated they caught the attention of every guy in the gym; and a collection of girls like me, the odds and ends. I caught sight of Daddy and waved my arms. He saw me and jogged up the steps.

"Ah. There she is," he said, spotting Mom. "Always in demand." He couldn't take his eyes off of her, and when she noticed him, her face lit up. She waved and blew kisses. I liked it when I caught those love looks that Mom and Dad had just for each other.

Before the game started, Mom came back to sit with us. She and Daddy cheered and rooted for Andy, who was, as promised, in the starting lineup. The coach kept him in for most of the first half until, as Daddy explained it, the team had enough of a lead to give their star player a rest.

Evan spent the entire first half standing in the doorway, leaning against the jamb. But he didn't take his eyes off the game for a second, and he even applauded when Andy made a three-pointer.

When had Evan become such an outsider, and why did Mom and Dad allow it? I knew what Mom always said: "And then there's Evan. He's always been . . . how should I put it? Our little challenge." Then she would give an exaggerated sigh, and Dad would nod in agreement. Andy the dream child, Evan the challenge, and Samantha the "darling" daughter, who doesn't know what she is yet.

"Want some popcorn?" Daddy asked me.

"Sure."

"She'll spoil her dinner," Mom warned.

"We'll share," Daddy said, handing me a dollar. "See if you can get Evan to come on up while you're at it."

I made my way down to the floor and wove through the milling crowd to the entrance. On purpose I bumped into Evan, who cracked a smile.

"Popcorn," I said, showing him the money. He followed me and then joined us in the bleachers. Daddy, Evan, and I polished off the bag of popcorn just as the half-time show was coming to an end. This time the show was a fifteen-minute version of the musical *Oklahoma!,* performed by the school's drama club.

Chapter 5

It turned out to be the four of us for dinner, since Andy wanted to celebrate the Panthers' first preseason win with his teammates. We ate at Louise's Café, which was actually the guesthouse of a lady named Betty. I don't know where the name "Louise" came from. Years ago, Betty had converted the house into a small restaurant. In the summers she served barbecue, and her customers sat out back at tables with red-checkered cloths and bottomless pitchers of lemonade. There were no menus, just a list on a chalkboard posted by the entrance.

"Looks like it's spaghetti and meatballs tonight," Daddy said.

"And spumoni for dessert," I added.

After eating, we were on our way to the car when a lady approached us. I didn't recognize her but figured it out fast when Evan cursed under his breath.

"Mr. and Mrs. Sheffield?"

"Yes?"

"I'm Sharon Porter, Evan's science teacher." She reached out to shake hands with our parents, and the meatballs became lead weights in the pit of my stomach.

"Is there a problem?" Mom asked.

Isn't there always a problem? I thought.

"I called earlier today. Did you get my message?" The meatballs in my stomach pitched and rolled. Dad looked at Mom, but she just shrugged and shook her head.

"Well, I'm glad I ran into you, because I really need to talk about some concerns I have."

Mom and Dad glared at Evan, who defiantly shook his head and tried to look like he had no idea what this could be about. There was a heavy moment of silence, during which Miss Porter fingered her necklace and red splotches bloomed on her neck. Maybe she didn't know this was nothing new.

"You said you have concerns," Daddy said.

"Uh . . ." Miss Porter, who was what Mom would call heavyset, swallowed hard, and her nostrils flared.

"He completes the labs in class, and he's actually really good at the hands-on activities we do, but he hasn't turned in any homework assignments. I think maybe he gets the labs done because the students work in groups for those."

"You mean he copies off of his lab partners," Daddy said, and Miss Porter didn't argue.

"Anything independent is incomplete. Let's just say he has a lot of 'the dog ate my homework' excuses. And lately, he's been rather disruptive."

Evan made a scoffing noise to object, but Mom snapped a look at him that scared me.

"Go to the car," she told us.

Evan started to argue. I was already three steps on my way when Daddy grabbed him by the arm and flung him in my direction. Evan quickly regained his composure and walked to the car as slowly as possible.

From the backseat, we looked to where the three were standing in the light of a streetlamp. They talked for what seemed like hours. Then they shook hands again, and Mom and Dad strode over to the car. I could feel their anger as they got in.

"I am so disappointed in you," Mom started. Evan made no sign that he had even heard her. "Here we go again. When will you learn?" Her words were like little darts. Dad, on the other hand, said nothing. I'm not sure which was worse.

"You called your teacher Miss Porker?"

Evan laughed. "She misunderstood me."

"This is no laughing matter, young man."

There was an angry silence. Usually when they had these arguments, I kept my mouth shut, but this time I didn't.

"Porter and Porker are pretty close," I pointed out. Mom's eyes widened, and Evan laughed even harder.

"You stay out of this, young lady."

I wondered why we always became "young man" and "young lady" when we were in trouble.

Mom turned back around in her seat and launched the final dart.

"You embarrass me." That knocked the smirk right off of Evan's face.

When we pulled into the garage, Dad told me to go to bed. I had to admit that I was glad my parents weren't interested in figuring out why they'd missed Miss Porter's call earlier in the day.

In my room I could hear everything.

"I'm sick and tired of this. Why can't you just behave in school? We give you everything you need. Do you have any idea how lucky you are?" Mom was almost shrieking.

I pressed my hands against my ears and stared at the plastic family arranged in my dollhouse—plastic people with painted smiles.

The yelling grew louder.

"I thought we settled this last year," Dad started. "Your teachers wanted to make you repeat eighth grade, but we didn't agree to that because you said you'd try harder. You promised you'd ask your teachers for help when you needed it. Maybe we made a mistake. Maybe you should have been kept back."

I crawled out to the hallway. I could see the three of them. Mom and Dad were standing facing Evan, who was on the couch with his arms wrapped around himself. He was fighting back tears.

Dad continued. "Things have to change."

How many times have I heard that before? I thought.

"We just want the best for you," Mom said.

"We want you to be successful, and to have every opportunity," Dad added.

To my surprise, Evan looked straight up and locked eyes with me. Jolted, I fell back into the darkness of the hallway and held my breath. I knew he was thinking what I was. Mom and Dad said all the right things, but that's as far as it ever went. Arguments like this one flared up, feelings got hurt, and then everything just evaporated, and we all went back to the usual.

"You're going to write a letter of apology to Miss Porter," Dad said.

"I already said sorry."

"That's not good enough."

"Yes it is!" Evan yelled.

"Don't yell at your father!"

"Shut up, Mom!" Evan yelled louder.

And then there was a commotion. Mom sobbed, and a cry of my own slipped out. I could hear Dad pulling Evan to the kitchen table. There was a ruffle of paper and the slap of a pen on the table.

"Write," Dad growled.

"It's late, Graham," Mom said with a sudden change in tone. Evaporating already?

"Kathy, please. Evan, get started."

Crouched on the floor of the dark hallway, I could picture Evan hunched over the paper with the pen gripped awkwardly in his hand, and Dad standing over him.

"Is that your best?" Dad asked after a few

moments. I was confused when I heard Mom plead with Daddy to leave Evan alone.

"Which is it, Kathy? Are we going to deal with this or not?" And then to Evan, "Write."

I moved toward the railing.

"I am!" Evan cried. He sounded like a little boy.

"You didn't even spell her name right! Come on! It's *P-o-r*! Not *P-r-o*!"

"Graham, don't!" Mom snapped. There was a streak of panic in her voice I'd never heard before.

"You're not trying!"

"Leave me alone! I'm doing what you said!" Evan pleaded with tears in his voice.

"Start again," Dad demanded.

"Stop it!" Mom became frantic, and in the middle of their yelling, I heard a chair topple, followed by the sound of pounding feet. I caught a glimpse of Evan's red face before he ducked into his room and slammed the door.

"Why did you do that?" Mom asked in a high-pitched voice.

Daddy sighed. "I can't stand by and watch him . . . fail."

"You didn't have to humiliate him," Mom said, and headed upstairs. I slipped back into my room and leaned against my closed door for a moment.

I sat in front of my dollhouse and dusted the roof and floors with my fingers. I picked up the family and held them in my hands. I set one son over next to my stuffed animals and the other son in his room. I stood the mom at the window in her bedroom and set the dad in front of the TV. Then I put the girl up in her room and imagined that if a giant peeled off the front of our house, this is what he'd see. I considered scratching their smiles off but decided against that for the time being.

The next morning I woke with a start. The sun was bright, and I wondered what time it was. I felt something poking me and pulled one of my dollhouse dolls out from under me. It was the other son, still smiling. I pitched it at the dollhouse and crawled out of bed, listening for signs of who was up and about.

When I opened my door and walked down the hall, I heard Mom and Dad talking. They mentioned Evan's name, and I couldn't resist eavesdropping. Stepping lightly, I moved toward their room and froze once when the creak of the wood floor echoed through the house. They went on talking.

"I did what I did last night to make a point," Daddy said.

"And what point was that?"

"Every year it's the same thing. We make demands, he promises to do better, and then he starts falling apart. Last week it was a fight. The week before that he cut school. He's not a bad kid. You know he does all of this because he struggles with learning. We can't let another year go by like this."

I could feel the sadness of Daddy's voice in my own heart and leaned closer to their door.

"I think we should go to the school and talk to someone before they call us in again or stop us on the street to tell us about another one of his stunts," he said.

"If we go talk to them, it's like we're admitting that we can't deal with our own kids. I won't do that," Mom said.

I could tell that they were getting dressed, because I could hear the padding of their feet on the floor as they moved about. The sounds of zippers and plumping of pillows told me I didn't have long to listen, but I didn't want to pull myself away just yet.

"I don't want people to think that we aren't good parents," Mom said.

"The fact that Evan struggles in school doesn't mean that we're bad parents. You're a wonderful mother. We give our children a good home, and that's why I think that we should go talk to his counselor at school. What can it hurt?"

"Do you remember the day we met?" Mom asked. I was confused by the change of subject and leaned closer to their door.

Dad chuckled and began the story I'd heard so many times. "You were a junior, and I was a senior."

"Star of the football team," Mom added, and then Daddy continued. "You were standing by the field: the most beautiful girl I'd ever seen. I went for a long pass, caught sight of you, and tripped over the water cooler."

"It was love at first sight." Usually, Mom laughed when she told this story, but this morning, I could hear tears in her voice.

The pad of Dad's feet became the clack of his shoes. Then all was still, and I imagined that he was hugging her.

What does this have to do with Evan and last night? I wondered to myself.

"Kathy, you're changing the subject."

Mom ignored this comment. "No, I'm not. School was a nightmare for me, and meeting you saved me." I perked up in surprise at a part of the story I'd never heard before. "When you graduated and then Andy came along, thank God for your parents. Mine were so . . ." She paused, and I pressed my ear against the door. "Cruel."

I flinched in surprise at the details of a story I thought I knew so well. "If it hadn't been for your parents . . ."

"Yes. But Evan doesn't have the same options you had," Daddy said.

"What's that supposed to mean?" Mom sounded angry.

What *was* that supposed to mean? I wondered, too.

Mom's quiet steps became stomps. She must have moved into their bathroom because her voice became hollow and her words were impossible to make out. I pressed my ear against their door to no avail.

"What are you doing?" All of a sudden Andy was crouched down behind me.

"Ugh!" I stifled a scream and clutched my chest in an effort to keep my pounding heart where it belonged.

Andy was delighted to catch me doing something I wasn't supposed to. I watched a smile light up his face, and then I heard Mom and Dad move toward the door and saw the doorknob begin to turn. All I could do was stand up and hope it looked like I just happened to be walking down the hall at the very same moment they were on their way out of their room.

"Oh," Mom said when she saw us. "Look who's up already."

I could tell that she was searching our faces for any signs that we had heard their conversation. I guess I had a good poker face because she flashed a grin and led the way downstairs. And then my family became its usual busy self.

"I've got errands to run today," Mom said.

"I'm off to the office. I've got paperwork from the week to catch up on." With a quick peck on Mom's cheek, Dad dashed out the door. Andy slung his gym bag over his shoulder, grabbed three blueberry muffins from the fridge, and headed out behind Dad, saying something about an early practice, even though they had won the night before.

"You'll need to fix yourself breakfast, honey. I've got to get going."

Mom grabbed her purse, checked her hair in the entry-hall mirror, and dashed out the door.

"Hey, Sam," Evan patted my head as he made his way past me and into the kitchen. He flipped on the radio and ducked into the pantry. He came out with a box of pancake mix in one hand and a bag of chocolate chips in the other. Humming to the radio, he searched the cabinets until he found the box of food coloring.

"Red, blue, or green?" he asked.

Did I imagine the night before? Evan seemed perfectly happy as he hummed to the music and began preparing his specialty, chocolate-chip pancakes. He held up the selection of colors and raised his eyebrows, waiting for me to make a choice. I just stared at him, speechless.

"Fine. Blue it is."

My eyes landed on the balled-up paper on the floor near the sink, and I saw Evan glance at it too.

"I'm supposed to write an apology. Like that's going to happen." He gestured toward a fresh piece of stationery and a blue ballpoint pen on the table. He poured the pancake mix into the bowl without measuring and added water from the tap. Somehow he always got it right. Then he squeezed three drops of the blue food coloring into the batter and stirred until it became a deep shade of ocean blue.

He tore the bag of chocolate chips open with his teeth and dumped the whole bag into the bowl. I noticed a faint bruise on his arm, and the scuffle between Dad and Evan flashed in my mind.

"Mix those in while I get the griddle ready." He handed me the bowl of pancake batter.

"Are you okay?"

"Sure," he said quickly without looking at me. I set the bowl on the table and stirred, watching Evan work. He loved to cook and was really good at it.

"I could help you write it."

He didn't respond.

"The letter. I could help," I offered again, and quickly regretted it when I saw a flash of anger in his eyes.

"Drop it." He turned up the radio and sang along with Billy Idol. He let the griddle get hot and then took the bowl from me.

"Get the plates and the chocolate syrup," he said, flipping the pancakes like a pro.

Chapter 6

"Let's go see Mrs. Brewster," I suggested, swallowing the last bite of my fourth pancake.

"Okay," Evan said. He rinsed the dishes while I got dressed. When I came down he was already out front on his bike. I pulled my bike out of the garage, and we headed to Mrs. Brewster's house at the top of Tea Lane.

We had met Mrs. Brewster about two years ago on a hot summer day. All we'd known about her before then was what Mom had told us. She was an angry, lonely woman. Angry because years ago she had been in a car accident that left her paralyzed from the waist down. Lonely because her husband and two children had died in the accident.

Evan and I had been walking home from getting ice cream in town when we saw Mrs. Brewster struggling to wheel herself up the steep hill toward her house. I felt a little nervous, but Evan walked right up to her.

"Do you need help?" he asked.

"Do I look like I need it?" she retorted in a strained voice, and I took a step back. Evan looked her over.

"Sort of," he admitted.

"No, honey, I do this every day." She groaned, and the muscles in her arms flexed in an effort to push herself up the hill. She inched forward and grunted. She shifted her gloved hands back on the wheels and pushed herself forward again. Little muscles quivered in her arms, and drops of sweat splashed onto her green pants like raindrops. Her gray hair was streaked with sweat, and her face was red. She was panting, but as she got closer to her house, she picked up speed, and with one final burst of energy she made it to the top of a long ramp at the side of the porch. She took deep breaths and wiped her face on her upper arms. She pulled her gloves off and tossed them onto a wicker table.

"Well, are you going to come visit with me or

not?" she asked, and I was startled when I realized that we had been staring at her the whole time.

At her invitation I immediately shook my head and started to walk away, but Evan grabbed my hand and pulled me along.

"You're Mrs. Sheffield's kids, right?"

"Yeah," Evan answered.

"You know, most people"—she was still breathing hard, so her words came out in spurts—"don't even ask if I need or want help. They just assume I do and start pushing me along. Makes me damn furious."

I looked at Evan with wide eyes, hoping he'd get the message that I did not want to stay. To my dismay he plopped down in the overstuffed floral print cushions of a white wicker chair across from Mrs. Brewster. I had no choice but to do the same, and I was struck by how comfortable it was.

On the table there was a thick leather-bound journal. It was the kind with a ribbon attached for saving your place. Her red ribbon was frayed and marked a place close to the end of the journal. I wondered what she wrote about. Her children? Did she write poems or stories? Sections of the newspaper were scattered about, and there were stacks of books. They had shiny plastic covers—library books. A chorus of birds chirped and chattered as they darted from one bird feeder to the next. There must have been a dozen feeders hanging from the low branches of the huge oak tree in her front yard.

"I love to read," she said, pointing to the books I'd already noticed. "And when I'm in the mood, I write sappy poetry." She laughed at herself and then continued. "In the house I have a special lift that gets me up and down the stairs. I cook for myself and my fat cat, Dudley. I feel and think like any other human being. People forget that when they see this chair." She pounded the armrests and looked at us. "So? What about you two?"

I was stunned, and my heart leaped into my throat. What could I say after that? My biggest problem was having a bedtime that was too early. Evan was grinning, and there was an excited light in his eyes.

"So?" she urged.

"We'll come see you tomorrow," Evan said.

We will? I almost blurted out loud.

"That will be excellent." Mrs. Brewster nodded.

We will? I thought again, looking from Evan to Mrs. Brewster.

"Mrs. Brewster?" Mom asked when I mentioned at dinner that we'd visited her. "She's not a very friendly person."

"And I'm sure she doesn't need you two underfoot," Daddy added.

"We weren't exactly underfoot," Evan pointed out.

"You know what your father means. Just stick to playing with your own friends."

"She reads a lot of books and she writes poetry and stuff," I said.

"Hmm," Mom said the way she does when she thinks something isn't very interesting or important.

"She wheels herself up Tea Lane. Do you know how steep that is? She gets herself to the top every day. She was sweating buckets, but she didn't quit."

"That's enough, honey. Eat your dinner," Daddy said.

"I'm just saying, she's pretty interesting and she invited Evan and me to . . ." All of a sudden I felt a foot pressing my foot and saw Evan flashing a warning with his eyes.

"To what?" Mom asked.

"Visit," I said in a small voice. Evan sighed with frustration.

"Well, that's very nice, but like your mother said, stick to playing with your own friends. Now eat."

"Are you coming?" Evan asked the next morning as he lugged a sack of trash out to the garbage cans.

When I hesitated, he shrugged and started down the driveway.

"Hold on," I called. "Bikes would be faster." And though our parents' words "Play with your own friends" nagged at me, I was wondering what sappy poetry sounded like and hoped she might share some.

Evan smiled, and we made our second trip to Tea Lane. This time, Mrs. Brewster had pound cake and pink lemonade ready for us. She pointed out the different birds that dined at the feeders in her yard. She knew the names of every one of them.

"So," Mrs. Brewster said one morning, "you haven't really told me about yourselves." Her words were like a challenge, and even though I had grown to trust Mrs. Brewster, I felt that same wave of panic I'd felt the first day. What did I have to say to a woman who was so smart and had suffered so much? I busied myself with a mouthful of pound cake and looked to Evan.

He sat up, chugged his chocolate milk, and looked her straight in the eyes. "I like to draw. I hate school. And it makes me damn furious when people assume that I want to follow in my brother's footsteps."

Mrs. Brewster and Evan grinned at each other

and nodded happily. For the rest of that summer, we visited Mrs. Brewster almost every morning.

"Boy, am I glad you're here today!" she said, waving from her porch. She dashed out her cigar in a nearby flowerpot. I giggled at this and decided that the next time we worked with clay in school, I would make her an ashtray. Shortly after we'd met, she had explained that when she was a girl, her older cousin had taught her how to smoke cigars. They used to go out behind the barn on their farm in Nebraska and smoke the afternoons away. One time her mom caught them, and she was sure she was going to get it. But her mom just peeked around the corner and, seeing that the coast was clear, asked for a light. She laughed herself to tears at this memory.

I settled onto the soft cushions of her wicker furniture and glanced at the books on her table. One called *The Grapes of Wrath* was lying open, facedown.

"What are grapes of wrath?" I asked, and she laughed and picked up the book.

"This is one of John Steinbeck's greatest books. I've read it so many times and each time it gets better." She actually hugged the book and gently set it on the table. I liked hearing her talk about books and especially enjoyed the days that she read to us. She put on voices that were just like the ones I imagined the characters would have, and she always stopped at the most exciting parts just to torture us with suspense until the next time we visited. I'll never forget the first time she read to us. It was *The Lion, the Witch and the Wardrobe,* and though I was sure I saw tears in Evan's eyes, he quickly brushed them away when he saw me looking at him and refused to talk about it later.

"So have you and Gilbert solved Mrs. Teedle's wig mystery?" she asked as she poured chocolate milk from a glass pitcher.

"No." I laughed.

Dudley brushed against my legs and then hopped up into my lap. I sputtered at tufts of gray fur that floated into my face as I stroked him from head to tail. Then he spied something in a bush and leaped away to investigate.

Mrs. Brewster was interested in everything we talked about. She was never critical and gave advice in a way that didn't feel like she was telling us what to do. The only subject we never discussed was her family. I asked about her children once, and her smile vanished. She told us to be on our way, and the next time we visited I knew enough not to bring up the subject again, even to apologize. Though I had to admit, it was always on my mind. Not because I wanted to hear gory details, but because I wondered how a person lived after losing her whole family.

"So, Evan, are you working on any new pieces?"

"A sketch. I want to enter it in the Lafayette Art Festival."

She clapped her hands and reached for a wooden case set beside her chair. Chuckling to herself, she struggled to pull it onto the table. She dusted it with her hands and worked the latch open. The hinges creaked and gave way. Evan's eyes lit up at the sight. Neatly tucked into each side of the case were colored pencils, charcoal pencils, quills, ink, brushes of all sizes, tubes of paint, disks of watercolors, sharpeners, and an array of rulers.

"I ordered this from a catalog a few years ago when I thought I might try my hand at being an artist. I don't know what I was thinking. I can't even draw a stick figure."

I knew how she felt. Whenever I drew something in class, my teachers would smile and say things like, "Well, Samantha, why don't you explain what you've drawn?" Or "My, you put a lot of effort into this, didn't you?" My drawings always ended up in the hard-to-see places in the classroom.

Evan ran his fingers over the art supplies.

"I bet you could put this to good use," Mrs. Brewster said. He nodded, not taking his eyes off the case. "You'll need some paper or canvas, or whatever you artists work on. I came to my senses before I ordered that from the catalog."

Evan beamed. She'd called him an artist.

At that moment I wished that time could stand still and I could sit there with Mrs. Brewster and Evan forever. It was so peaceful.

Later that afternoon Mom wrangled me into going grocery shopping with her. We were winding our way through the store when we ran into one of her Women's Guild friends in the cereal aisle.

"By the way," her friend said. "I was talking to Susan, who said you didn't RSVP for next Tuesday's city council meeting."

Mom looked confused. "Why would I do that? We don't have anything planned that I know of." Now it was her friend's turn to look confused.

"Didn't you get the letter? The members of the Guild are being recognized at the next city-council meeting. Each of us is being honored with a City Service Award!" Her friend laughed. "Isn't that great?"

Mom's face flushed. "Yeah, great. My letter

must have gotten lost in the mail," she said. "I'll call first thing Monday. Thank you, Donna. Come on, Samantha."

"That's great, Mom," I said as she led the way to the next aisle. "Oh, Mom, can we get this? I had it at my friend Gabby's house once." I pulled a box of Hamburger Helper, off the shelf.

"No."

"But it tastes good, and"—I turned the box over—"it's simple. It says to brown . . ."

"I said no," Mom snapped, and hurried down the aisle. I returned the box and caught up with her.

I was confused by her reaction to what should have been good news, but I didn't get a chance to ask about it before she sent me to pick up a bottle of dish soap. "Get the green kind. It smells the best," she said.

"Joy or Dawn?" I asked.

"The green one, honey. You know the kind I use." She moved on, and I completed my mission.

"Aren't you happy about the award?" I asked on the way home.

"Sure."

"You don't seem very happy."

"What do you want me to do? Break into a song and dance?" she snapped.

"I'm just saying. Jeez." I dropped the subject and gazed out the window.

At dinner that night Mom shared her news with everyone else.

"It's Tuesday night," she said, smiling, more like herself. "They're giving everyone in the Women's Guild an award for starting the Clean Park Program."

"That's wonderful, honey," Dad said.

"Way to go, Mom," Andy added. I gave her a hug. Evan kept right on cutting his pork chop.

"I was thinking we could go dress shopping tomorrow."

"I have to wear a dress?"

"Of course. This is a very special occasion. The boys will wear dress shirts and ties." Evan was still cutting away, and Andy nodded.

"But I don't want to wear a dress."

"This isn't about what you want," Daddy said.

"Yeah, Sam," Evan suddenly piped up. "It's all about making Mom look good."

Big mistake. Mom's mouth dropped open. Dad threw his napkin down. "Go to your room," he said.

Evan looked down at his uneaten dinner and

started to pick up his plate, but Daddy grabbed it, spilling some in the process, and made him leave it behind.

"Ahh, another delightful dinner, thanks to Evan," said Andy. His comment was punctuated by the slam of Evan's door. Andy announced that he was going out with friends and excused himself. He gave Mom a kiss on the cheek, told her he was proud of her, and headed out to his car.

Mom dabbed at her eyes with her napkin and went out to the porch swing.

"Do the dishes," Daddy said to me as he got up to join Mom.

Later that night I woke when I heard a noise downstairs. I got up to investigate and found Evan in the kitchen. By the light of the refrigerator, he was eating leftovers.

"Did I wake you?"

I nodded. He didn't apologize. He let the refrigerator close, and the full moon was bright enough for us to see without any other lights. We sat at the table, and I watched Evan polish off the rice and pork chops. He put the empty Tupperware back in the fridge and then pulled out the Rocky Road ice cream. I grabbed two spoons and joined him for a midnight treat.

"I didn't mean to hurt her feelings."

"Then why did you?"

Evan licked his spoon. "I don't know," he said. "She just acts so perfect all the time, and she's not."

"I don't understand," I said, wanting him to explain, but he just leaned back in his chair out of the moonlight so I couldn't see his face. Then I got a brain freeze and dropped my spoon in the nearly empty tub. "Ugh," I groaned and massaged the bridge of my nose. Evan took one more bite and put the ice cream away.

"I'm not going to that ceremony," he said.

"You have to."

"G'night," Evan said, and he left me alone. I sat at the table for a while and listened to how loud the tick-tock of the grandfather clock was when the house was dark and still. My brain freeze faded away, and I went back to bed.

Mom and I did go dress shopping at the Mervyn's over in Lafayette, and on Tuesday night I put on my new green dress and shiny black shoes. I had picked a yellow-and-white dress, but Mom pointed out that it wasn't fashionable to wear white shoes after Labor Day, and white shoes were the only thing that would go with a yellow-and-white dress. Never mind the fact that I usually hated dresses and had managed to find one I actually liked.

"Don't you look darling!" Mom exclaimed when I joined Andy, Mom, and Dad downstairs. I didn't feel darling and pulled at the scalloped collar around my neck. Everyone was dressed and ready to go—everyone except Evan, who was not home yet.

"Did he say anything to either of you?" Mom asked Andy and me.

"No," Andy said. I kept quiet about the other night, but I had to wonder if anyone was really surprised.

"He knew we had to leave by six fifteen. It's nearly that now!" Mom said, close to tears. Dad paced by the front door and stopped abruptly when Evan came walking up.

"Evan!" Dad shouted, whipping open the front door. "Where have you been?"

Evan raced upstairs without so much as a glance at Daddy and returned momentarily in the dress shirt Mom wanted him to wear. His tie was hanging loose around his neck, and in the car Andy tied it for him.

We made it to City Hall just in time to see Mom's friend, Glenda, receive her plaque. Donna had already received hers and was all smiles. She'd saved seats for us and waved like a wild woman when we entered. Then it was Mom's turn. Dad, Andy, Evan, and I stood beside her as the mayor read a long list of the ways she contributed to the town.

"Mrs. Sheffield is also one of Orinda's shining stars. We honor her tonight for her work with the Women's Guild, of course, but also for her work with the Clean Park Program, the Garden Committee, and the PTA at the high school and elementary school. One wonders how she does it all."

Mom stood tall with a bright smile on her face, listening carefully.

"Kathy, we are pleased to present you with this plaque, just a small token of our appreciation for all that you do."

Mom turned toward the audience and gave a slight nod. They applauded, and like a model on the catwalk, she walked over to the mayor's podium. She shook his hand, and then she wedged herself in between Daddy and me to pose for pictures. So many flashes went off as pictures were taken that every time I blinked I saw blue spots.

At home Mom set her plaque on the mantle over the fireplace next to her Green Thumb trophy, and Daddy surprised her with cake and ice cream. He had ordered a cake with "Congratulations, Kathy" written in cursive. It was yellow and white, and I figured yellow-and-white cakes must be okay after Labor Day because Mom didn't say anything about that.

On my way to bed later that night, I stopped by Evan's room. He was on the floor with his desk lamp beside him. His fingers were black from the piece of charcoal he was using. He looked up at me, grinned, and went back to work.

"It's beautiful," I said, gazing at his sketch of a herd of wild horses running across an open plain. Their manes waved in the wind, and there was fierceness in their eyes. The lead stallion had muscles that knotted and rippled beneath his coat. Toward the back of the herd, there was a foal with its mother at its side. She was its protector and guide across the open land.

I crouched down for a closer look. With ease, Evan added lines and details that made the sketch even more amazing. There were rocky mesas, and in the distance thunderclouds loomed.

"I'm glad you came tonight."

Evan just shrugged and concentrated on his work.

"It meant a lot to Mom," I added.

He set the charcoal in a little pouch and carefully propped his sketch against the side of his dresser. A whole collection of sketches and paintings nearly filled his closet. They were on everything from actual sketch paper to napkins, the backs of flyers, and the tattered envelopes of junk mail. He brushed off his hands and told me to go to bed.

On my way to my room, I stopped in the hallway and could hear Mom and Dad talking downstairs. "In honor of Katherine Sheffield for her dedicated service to the community," Daddy said, reading her the inscription on the plaque, and then I heard soft music, the slow kind that only they liked, and imagined them dancing. I sat in the hall for a moment, listening to the light scuff of their feet on the floor, the music, and the rustle of papers in Evan's room. Then I headed to bed, unable to understand why I felt a kind of sad heaviness on what should have been a happy evening.

Chapter 7

The next day while I was supposed to be doing homework, I watched Mom cooking dinner. It looked like another casserole. I thought it would turn out a lot better if she used a cookbook. She said she didn't need to, that she'd learned how to cook from her great-grandma who'd never owned a cookbook and used to cook for all the miners in a mining camp up north.

"You get it right by tasting along the way," she explained. I wasn't so sure about that.

Evan sat across the table from me with a book, some notebook paper, three ballpoint pens, a pencil, and a ruler. He looked tense and was moving his lips as he pointed to each word in the book. Mom glanced at him a couple of times, sighed, bit her lip, and, with a quick shake of her head, went back to work.

I focused on my world history assignment and tried to ignore the nagging guilt I felt as I breezed through pages of reading while Evan seemed stuck on the same page.

"Mom, can you help me with this?" I asked when I came to a question about Mesopotamia.

"You know your Daddy is better at that. Ask him when he gets home. He loves that stuff," she said, slipping into the pantry.

"Ask your father" was her usual answer when any of us asked for help on homework, unless it was math. Mom was a whiz at arithmetic. She could add really big numbers in her head, and she made long division look like a cinch.

"Dad's been late every night this week," Evan said. "Maybe you should help her now. . . ."

"He called earlier. He'll be home normal time," Mom said quickly and ducked into the pantry again. She came out with a couple of bottles of spices and busied herself with opening and smelling each one. When she found one she liked, she returned the others to the spice rack.

"Hey." Andy came through the door, flung his gym bag toward the stairs, and poured himself a tall glass of orange juice. He sat at the table, and I noticed Evan hunch over his work even more, like he didn't want Andy to see him struggling. It was so different from how he looked when he was drawing—tall, confident, strong.

When dinner was ready, Evan and I cleared our books from the table while Daddy changed out of his work clothes. We were just digging into the concoction of a casserole Mom had prepared when Daddy mentioned that the school had called him at work. Evan's shoulders fell, and he started to get up from the table, but Daddy put a hand on his arm and told him to stay put.

"What now?" Mom asked.

"The counselor talked to me about having Evan tested for a learning disability. We've discussed this before, and I really think it's a good idea."

I felt a bubble of hope as Mom slowly chewed her mouthful. She swallowed, put her fork down, and simply said, "No."

The bubble popped.

"Why not?" Daddy asked. Evan tried to escape again, but Daddy held him back.

"What are they going to find out that we don't already know? We know our children better than some school counselor." Her voice was pinched. "Remember his fourth-grade teacher? She wanted to have him tested for a learning disability, too. Come to think of it, so did his third-grade teacher, or was it second-grade?"

"Maybe we should have taken their advice then," Daddy said softly.

"Graham! Where is this coming from? We've always agreed. From the time Evan was in first grade and his teacher wanted him to repeat the year because he was . . . how did she put it? Slower than the other kids. Remember that? I'll never forget the know-it-all look on her face. We've always agreed that keeping him back wasn't the right thing to do, and Mrs. Teedle even said so. The year Evan had her, she talked about how all the research says that holding slower students back isn't really good for them."

The way Mom kept using the word "slower" made my stomach turn. Evan slumped farther in his seat.

"Yeah." Andy joined in the conversation, and Evan flashed an angry glare at him. "High school's hard enough. I mean, it's not like Evan's a star athlete or part of any cool group, and he's already in dumbbell English. Nobody repeats in high school. They just drop out."

Daddy grimaced at Andy's comments, and Mom suddenly looked sick, like she might even throw up. She closed her eyes and massaged her temples.

"I'm not talking about having Evan repeat a grade in high school, Katherine," Daddy got up from his seat and walked over to Mom. "I really think we're at a point now where we need to listen to what the teachers and counselors have to say. If they do whatever testing they're suggesting, maybe they'll find a reason why Evan struggles so much and then we can deal with it." Daddy put a hand on Mom's shoulder. "Together."

"Could you stop talking about me like I'm not even here? And you, shut up!" Evan shouted at Andy.

"I'm just trying to help," he said.

"Be quiet," Mom snapped, having recomposed herself. "Evan, I know that school is difficult for you. If you could just apply yourself and stay out of trouble, it wouldn't be so hard."

Daddy interrupted, "We've tried everything. Tutors, whatever supplies he needs, dictionaries, organizers . . . We even got him checked for glasses, for crying out loud. I really think it's time to try something else." He walked back to his seat.

Aren't you a little late? I thought.

"I don't want people to think . . ." Mom stopped, and tears glistened in her eyes.

"Think what?" Daddy asked. She gulped and blinked back tears.

"That it's my fault that our son is . . ." She stopped and looked at him.

Evan's face flushed. "What?" he demanded. "Dumb? Stupid? Huh? What is it, Mom?"

She didn't say yes or no, and he looked at her with wide eyes. She reached out to him, but Evan avoided her touch. This wasn't the kind of hurt that she could kiss and make better. He pushed away from the table, ran to his room, and slammed the door.

"Nice, Katherine," Daddy said.

"Those were his words," Mom said as if that made it all okay. She got up and stood at the sink. Then she started clearing the table.

"I'm not finished eating yet!" Andy whined, and grabbed a hold of his plate. "God! Doesn't anyone care about what's going on in *my* life? Do you even know that I'm up for Homecoming King?"

"Really?" Mom asked in a voice fluttery with hope. Andy sulked, and at that moment, it took all of my strength not to haul off and throw my plate at him.

Daddy got up and went out to work in the garage. He had a small workbench where he made things like birdhouses and mailboxes. He took them to work and sold them on his lunch breaks. I left the table too.

In my room I scooped the mom doll out of my dollhouse. Then I opened the window, stood her on the ledge and, as if flicking a marble, I sent her flying. It was too dark to see where she landed. I was peering down at the shrubs when a light caught my eyes.

It came from Evan's room. Then I heard the window slide open, and he climbed out. I watched him move across the ledge to the rain gutter. As soon as he started making his way down the downspout, he was covered in complete darkness, and I could only hear him land with a thud and then tramp through the overgrown grass of our backyard into the woods.

I stood there in shock. Was he running away? Who could blame him? Should I tell Mom and Dad? I could hear the buzz of Dad's power tools and the blast of a train whistle in the distance.

Then I heard a light knock on Evan's door. "Evan?" Mom asked, and my heart stopped. I didn't want to imagine what would happen if she found out that Evan wasn't in his room.

"Evan? Can I talk to you?" she tried again.

"Mom?" I called in hopes of distracting her.

"What, honey?" She came to my doorway. I was startled by how weary she looked.

"Can you tuck me in and . . ."

"And?" she asked.

"Sit with me for a while?"

"Okay," she said with a small smile. At the very least I figured I'd bought Evan some time. I put on my pajamas while she turned down my covers. Then I climbed into bed and scooted over to make room for her. She settled onto my bed slowly and carefully as if she was afraid she might break it.

"Comfy?" she asked as she put her arms around me. I nodded, but it was a lie. Every muscle in my body was tense, and all I could think about was what she had said about Evan. I could feel her heart beating way too fast, and her hands were cold. Her hair fell over my face, and then I felt a tear.

She quickly wiped at it, but more followed. "I'm a mess," she said in a strained voice. "Honey, don't let what happened at dinner upset you. And . . ." She paused like she was choosing her words carefully. "This is something you need to keep to yourself."

"What do you mean?"

"Don't get to talking with your friends about it. This is personal family business that we need to deal with . . . privately."

This brought tears to my own eyes, and for a moment I thought I was going to lose my casserole right then and there.

The whine of Dad's power saw sounded then, and I couldn't decide who I was angrier with. Daddy for burying himself away with his birdhouses or Mom for caring more about what others thought of her than helping her own son.

Mom saw my tears. "Sweet girl, don't worry. We'll work things out." She got up and reached for the light switch.

"Leave it on," I said quickly.

She looked at me. "Okay." She smoothed my covers, cupped my face with her hands, and wished me sweet dreams.

Was she serious? She left me alone then, and I was so angry it made me hot. I kicked off my covers and checked to make sure she'd given up on talking to Evan. I looked down the hall in time to catch a glimpse of her bedroom door closing. Then I put my clothes back on and leaned out my window again. I could see the eaves of the roof where I could get a good foothold. I figured I could sidestep over to the trellis, which was like a ladder covered in vines. It must have been secured to the house in some way or it would blow down in storms.

I climbed out my window. I told myself not to look down, but with each step, beads of sweat broke out on my upper lip. My mouth was dry and my knees were weak. I held my breath until I made it to the trellis, and then I slowly let it out, hugging the trellis for a moment to get up the nerve for the rest of my descent.

Step by step I made it down, then ran into the dark woods. We had played hide-and-seek in these woods a million times, so even in the dark I knew my way around. I wasn't afraid of the dark, although daylight would have been nicer.

"Evan?" I whispered, and moved deeper into the woods. I came to a path that was a fire-access road and followed it for a while. My eyes had adjusted to the darkness, so I could see pretty well by the light of the moon.

"Evan?" I called again, and then stopped to listen. I walked on, and then I heard, "What the hell?" and felt a rush of relief.

Evan ran up to me. "What are you doing? How did you get down here?" He looked behind me.

"I sneaked out just like you." I sat down on a log and looked up at him.

Evan groaned and slapped his forehead. "You shouldn't have done that," he said, sitting down next to me. "You could have fallen."

"Are you running away or something?"

"I thought about it, but where could I go, and how would I get there even if I did have a place to go?"

"That was real bad tonight," I blurted.

He picked up a handful of little rocks and threw them one at a time. Some hit trees, making a sharp knocking sound, and landed with a thud in the dirt.

Then, in a voice thick with sadness, he said, "Don't they think that if I could do good in school, I would?" He pitched the last rock so hard, its knock echoed loud enough to send some night creature scurrying off, rustling the bushes as it darted away.

Silence settled back in along with the cold, and my teeth started to chatter.

"Here." Evan pulled off his sweatshirt and gave it to me. He was left with a T-shirt, but he said he wasn't cold.

"You're not dumb," I said.

Evan shrugged. "That's what you think."

"Evan . . ."

"Forget it. You can't fix this."

"So what do we do now?" I asked.

"Wait for everyone to go to bed, and then use the Hide-a-Key."

"That's how you got in that night?"

"Yup. It's easier than climbing back up."

We could see the house from where we sat. It looked big and warm.

"Come on," Evan said, pulling me to my feet. We walked along the fire road farther away from the house. The deeper into the woods we got, the darker it became.

Everything looked and sounded different in the dark. The constant chirp of crickets and the desperate croak of the last few frogs of the summer sounded so loud. All of a sudden Evan stopped. He put a finger to his lips and crouched down, pulling me down too, then looked at the sky.

"What are we looking for?" I asked, but he shushed me and pointed toward the tops of the trees.

"Falling stars?" I asked. He shushed me again and shook his head.

"Watch over there," he whispered. It was cold enough to see our breath in white puffs.

I looked and waited. Despite the cold, I couldn't get enough of the rich pine scent of the forest and the musty smell of dirt and fallen pine needles. I thought of the times I'd seen deer walk through these woods, so close to our house. I knew that all around us there were night animals watching us from their secret hiding spots.

I looked at Evan, whose eyes were fixed on the starry night sky, when all of a sudden, three giant owls glided overhead. They were silent and grand, and they took my breath away. Their wings were silvery white in the light of the full moon. They were peaceful and powerful, even playful as they gracefully dipped and swooped through the air, then vanished beyond the tops of the tall pines.

"Did you see that?" I asked, gripping Evan's sleeve and shaking it. I turned every which way, trying to spot them again.

"I see them almost every time I come here. They have nests somewhere close by."

"Will they fly back?"

"Not tonight," Evan said. He lay back and looked up at the sky. "They're off to hunt."

I stood and ran a couple of yards in the direction they'd flown, pine needles crunching under my feet. A twig snapped as I came to a stop, and all I could see in the sky were stars and the moon beginning to dip below the trees. I closed my eyes, and in my mind I could see the owls sweeping over the trees, joyfully free.

I knew that I had to see those owls again. I opened my eyes and looked back at Evan, who was settled on the ground. Somehow the owls made all the bad things that had happened that night disappear for just a while.

Chapter 8

We were quiet for a long time, and then Evan said softly, "I can't read." I wasn't sure I'd heard him right and looked over at him. He didn't repeat what he'd said, and he did not look at me.

I felt dizzy and suddenly exhausted. All I could think of was Evan straining over a book, pointing at words, moving his lips. I felt like crying.

"When I look at the pages, the letters spin, and I know this sounds weird, but sometimes the words actually slide off the page." His voice cracked. "I've always just gotten by, but I can't do it anymore." Tears were streaming down his face.

I was trying to imagine it. I thought back on times when I had sat with Evan at the kitchen table, doing homework. I remembered watching Daddy try to help him. He seemed to tower over Evan, who sat beside him, stumped and flustered by Daddy's growing impatience.

"Read it again," Daddy would say. "Try reading a little faster." And Evan would try. "You know that word. We just read it," Daddy would say when Evan faltered. I guess Daddy thought this was encouraging. Of course, Andy always picked those moments to announce that he'd gotten an A on a test or that he'd outscored the team in practice that day. Daddy would beam with pride, and Evan would wilt away like a stepped-on flower.

Sometimes the effort made Evan break into a sweat. Andy teased him about it once, and Evan socked him in the mouth. This landed Evan in his room for the night. Mom said that if he wasn't such a hothead he'd concentrate better, and it would all get easier.

"We have to get you help," I said.

"You heard Mom. Forget it. When I'm sixteen, I'm going to . . ." He stopped himself and wiped his eyes.

"Drop out?" My throat tightened. I sat up and looked at him.

"Never mind. You don't have to worry about it."

"That's exactly what Mom said earlier tonight. You're just like her!"

I got up and started running through the woods. I was surprised at how soon the house came into sight. Evan was right behind me and grabbed the back of my shirt.

"Wait!" he whispered, and then peered up at the house. It was dark and silent. "Okay. It's safe to sneak in," he declared. But before we started back, he told me to forget what he'd said.

"I mean it. And don't tell anyone about the reading or anything about tonight."

I didn't respond.

"Promise." There was a desperation in his voice I'd never heard before. I moved forward, but he grabbed me. "Samantha, you have to promise."

"Okay. I won't say anything."

We crept up the front steps, and just as he had said, there was a Hide-a-Key behind the porch light. Silently, we slipped inside and up to our rooms. There was no way I could possibly sleep, and sure enough, I watched the sun rise over the woods.

No one spoke at breakfast. Daddy headed to work early, and Mom was in the usual rush, which was fine with me, because unless it was "I'm sorry about last night," I couldn't imagine what she would say.

After school, Gilbert and I went to B&B Pharmacy. It had the best candy selection in town, and we were both carrying our allowances. I had $3.00. That's what Gilbert used to get, but when his parents split up, his Mom upped it to $5.00. Gilbert figured it was to make him feel better about the divorce and all. I don't know if it made him feel better, but he sure did manage to buy a lot of candy.

We were carefully considering each type of candy when something else caught my eye. Just beyond the candy section there was a whole shelf devoted to press-on nails. There were plain ones you could paint, and for just a bit more, there were sets of nails already painted. I looked at the packs of nails, and they seemed easy enough to put on.

"You're crazy," Gilbert said when he saw that I was going to pay $2.79 for a pack of purple press-on nails. He was holding a giant jawbreaker and a king-size candy bar, trying to decide which one he wanted.

"Go for the chocolate," I said, thinking that he could give me a piece of it, whereas there'd be no sharing licks on a jawbreaker. He knew me too well, because he returned the candy bar to the rack.

"I'm going to count how many licks it takes to get to the center," he said.

"And you think I'm crazy?" I looked at Gilbert, who laughed like a madman and crossed his green eyes, which were magnified behind his thick, round glasses.

That's what I liked best about Gilbert. He had looks only a mother could love; the worst asthma a person could have; food allergies; angry, divorced parents who fought about everything under the sun; bullies that hassled him at school; and he just kept on smiling.

He picked out a pack of licorice ropes, ten pieces of bubblegum, the kind that had comics and fortunes inside the wrappers, and three Abba-Zabas. It was a good thing he wasn't allergic to candy.

I followed him to the register with my fake nails.

"You're really serious?" he asked.

I nodded and paid for my new beauty experiment.

Up in Gilbert's tree house, we got started on our projects. Gilbert was very systematic. He figured he would lick ten times and make a tally mark on the wall of his tree house. I read the directions carefully and opened the package of nails. There was a little bottle of glue that reminded me of rubber cement. The smell of it stung my nostrils. The nails came in sets of five. I had to twist and snap them off the plastic mold.

"Eight . . . nine . . . ten," Gilbert announced, and made a hatch mark on the wall with his pocketknife. His tongue was green.

I brushed the glue on my pinky nail on my right hand and pressed the smallest nail into place. The directions said to hold for thirty seconds. I did this and moved on to my ring, middle, and index fingers. Finally I glued the largest nail to my thumb.

"Check it out," I said, fanning myself with my right hand. Gilbert furrowed his brow in deep concentration. He held up one finger, gesturing for me to hold on a moment, and licked three more times. He made his sixth notch and sighed like he was tired from all the hard work.

"So?" I asked, wiggling my new purple nails. He stared at them and then reached out to test how sharp the points were. I guess he was impressed, because he nodded and watched me get to work on my left hand.

This was a bit of a challenge, because I was left-handed and had to use my right hand to brush on the glue. My new nails kept getting in the way. Gilbert soon lost interest and went back to work on his jawbreaker. My right hand was shaky and uncoordinated.

I dropped a gob of glue and Gilbert stopped licking long enough to tell me not to get that girl stuff on his tree-house floor.

"Help me out, then," I said, holding the bottle out to him. He licked one more lick, made a tally mark, and carefully set his jawbreaker on its wrapper. I held out my left hand, and Gilbert swiped my pinky with glue.

"Here." I handed him the pinky nail, which he scrutinized for a moment. "Quick, before the glue dries," I said. He pressed the nail into place and held it for thirty seconds as I had instructed. My left hand was finished in a matter of minutes, and I was pleased with the results.

"Hey, they gave you some extras," Gilbert said, noticing a couple of purple nails still in the package.

"Want to try one on?" I offered.

"No, thanks," he said as he gathered up his jaw-breaker.

"You're going to wear a hole in your tongue," I said. It was green-black straight down the center. Gilbert shook his head and tossed a piece of Bazooka gum my way. I did not catch it. Not because it was a bad toss, but because my new nails got in the way. They clashed and clicked. It took me three tries to pick it up, and opening it was nearly impossible. I could see that Gilbert found this very entertaining. I ignored his stare and enjoyed the comic on the wrapper.

"Hey, Gilbert, my fortune says that wealth will come to me in many ways."

"Six . . . seven . . . eight . . ." He focused on his jawbreaker. "That's what they all say."

"See ya," I said, deciding it was time to go home. I dropped the rope ladder, tucked the nail glue and extra nails in my pocket, and sat with my feet dangling through the hole in the floor.

I stepped down and then reached for the sides of the ladder. I had done this a million times, but all of a sudden it felt completely different. Each time I gripped the ropes, my nails dug into my palms. But if I loosened my grip, I felt like I might fall. It was slow going, and every step of the way I was afraid that I would catch a nail or, even worse, break one off.

"A jawbreaker experiment would have been a lot easier," Gilbert pointed out once I'd made it to the ground.

I blew a big bubble and waved with both hands. All the way home I admired my work, holding my hands out, twisting and waving them like a model.

"Hi, Daddy," I greeted when I got home and

found him standing at the kitchen counter. He was looking through the phone book. I displayed my hands and posed, batting my eyes for added effect. He looked at me with a half smile and did not notice my nails.

"How does pizza with the works sound?"

I gave up my pose. "Good. Except no olives."

"Okay." He glanced down at the phone book. Impulsively I shot my hand out and splayed my fingers on the page.

"Sa . . ." Then he saw my nails and frowned. "What did I say about makeup?"

"These aren't makeup, and don't they look pretty?"

He eyed me for a moment and then moved my hand away so he could read the number.

I went to look for Evan and found him hard at work on another sketch. This one was of the owls. He had only just begun, but already he had captured their grace and beauty.

He looked up at me with a smile in his eyes. "I'm going to enter this one in the Lafayette Art Festival."

"Not the one with the horses?"

"Naa. I think the owls will turn out better."

I couldn't wait any longer, and in my most dramatic pose I leaned over and propped my elbows on his desk. Then I rested my chin in my hands and wiggled my fingers.

"Whoa!" He grabbed my hands for a closer look. By the light of his desk lamp, lumps and strings of glue that ran along my cuticles were suddenly much more obvious.

"Aren't they great?"

"Uh . . . sure." He was not very convincing. I sat on his bed and fanned my hands out on his blue bedspread. He must have seen my disappointment.

"They're nice," he said with more conviction. "Really."

"Gilbert helped me put the nails on my left hand," I said.

"You're kidding." Evan laughed.

"I think he did a pretty good job," I said.

Evan grabbed my left hand and inspected Gilbert's work more closely. He laughed again, but I was too happy to let it get to me. Maybe I couldn't do makeup, but I was a natural at nails.

"Where's Mom?" I asked as Andy, Evan, Daddy, and I sat down to dinner.

"She's at a Women's Guild meeting. They're hosting the Thanksgiving dinner at a mission in Oakland this year. She got a catering business to donate their cooking services. We're all going to volunteer," Daddy said, serving me a plate of pizza.

We used to go to our grandparents' house for Thanksgiving. Grandma and Grandpa Sheffield lived in Southern California in one of those fifty-five-and-older senior-citizen complexes. They were the only grandparents we knew, since Mom and her parents had what Mom called a "falling out" back before Andy was born. All I knew of her parents was what I got through pictures and a couple of stories she told about when she was a little girl.

Three years ago our grandparents moved to Florida. Grandpa Sheffield said he was excited about striking out on an adventure. Daddy was really upset and argued that there was plenty of adventure in Southern California. Mom was sad too, because Grandma and Grandpa Sheffield were more like parents to her than her own had ever been. I was also disappointed, because they did live near all the good amusement parks. The closest we came to an amusement park in our part of Northern California was when the carnival came to Lafayette, and even then Mom never let us go on the rides, because she said they weren't safe.

Ever since they had moved, we got cool gifts

in the mail for Christmas and cards with pictures of the two of them standing hand in hand on the beach. They decided that they couldn't afford to travel out to California every year and promised that they would come to each of our high-school graduations.

With no other major family nearby, and since Mom didn't like to cook, she threw herself into doing charity work for Thanksgiving and dragged us along. Last year Mom's garden society delivered Thanksgiving meals to elderly people who lived alone. Andy was excited about that one, because he had just gotten his license and got to drive one of the delivery vans. The year before that, the Women's League delivered blankets to a nursing home. Mom made fifteen blankets that year.

"We're going to serve meals to homeless people on Thanksgiving?" Andy asked.

"Yes. Your mother is really excited. You know cooking's not her strong point." He stopped and looked at me with a devilish grin. "Don't tell her I said that."

"I won't," I promised.

"This way she gets to do her committee work, and we get to share a meal with those who are less fortunate. I think sometimes we forget that we have it pretty good in this house."

"This is going to look great on my college applications," Andy pointed out.

Evan rolled his eyes as he stuck a piece of pepperoni followed by a foot-long string of cheese into his mouth. He reeled in the steaming cheese and grabbed another piece of pepperoni.

"Eat up, honey," Daddy said to me, reaching for a second piece.

I was faced with a challenge. How could I pick up my pizza to eat it? First, I tried using just my nails like tongs or tweezers, but I felt them start to pull away and quickly dropped my pizza. Then I tried lifting the piece with one hand and sliding the whole thing onto my other hand. I sat with the piece on my palm and tried taking a bite. This worked until Andy asked, "What are you doing?"

I froze midbite. I had my right hand palm-up like a waiter carrying a tray of food.

"Eating. What does it look like?" I asked with my mouth full.

"That's rude. Act like a lady," Daddy scolded.

I slid what was left of my pizza back onto my plate and tried another approach. I picked up a fork with the insides of my thumb and forefinger and jabbed at my pizza. All of a sudden I fumbled the fork, and my left thumbnail flipped up into the air, landing on Evan's plate.

"What the . . ." Andy squinted and looked at the purple nail.

"Damn it!" I cried.

"Samantha!" Daddy snapped.

Andy started laughing when he finally figured it out. "Fake nails?"

I snatched the nail from Evan's plate and ran upstairs, where I locked myself in the bathroom, Andy's laughter trailing me. Daddy said something that quieted him briefly. Then I heard chair legs scoot along the kitchen floor and heavy footsteps up the stairs.

"Samantha?" It was Daddy.

I didn't answer.

"Honey, come finish eating."

"I can't!" I sobbed and looked at my nails. I had pizza sauce under most of them and a piece of mushroom skewered on my right pinky nail. Then I noticed that the middle finger nail on my left hand was missing altogether. This set off a whole new round of sobs.

"Can I help you with something?"

This made me cry and laugh at the same time. I could just picture my dad giving me a manicure. "No."

"I'll wrap up some pizza for you, and maybe Mom can help you when she gets home."

Daddy left me alone, and after a few minutes, I heard Andy go into hysterics again. He must have found my other nail. I gave my nails one last look, and then I pried each one off, letting them land in the sink. Plink . . . Plink . . . Plink. They had lasted just over three hours, and I was back to my own short, gnarled nails. Nail-biting was one nervous habit I just couldn't break, no matter how much Mom nagged me.

"Sam?" It was Evan. I stared at my pile of nails. "Do you need this?"

He poked my missing nail under the door. It wobbled back and forth on the bathroom tile. Again I cried and laughed at the same time.

"Thanks," I said, picking it up. "But," I opened the door. "I give up."

Evan looked in the sink. "It's probably just as well. They seem like a lot of trouble."

I gathered up my nails and took them to my room where I put them in my jewelry box. Later that night, Mom used a special kind of remover on cotton balls to get the rest of the glue off my fingers. Of course she took the opportunity to point out that if I didn't bite my own nails, I wouldn't need fake ones.

Chapter 9

Homecoming was a big deal in Orinda. Of course, Mom was head of the decorating committee for the dance, which was to be held in the high-school gym.

"It's a futuristic theme," she said as we drove over to the gym the Friday before the dance. I had been recruited to help decorate. It was fun to see the moms transform the huge, sweaty hall into a ballroom.

"Glenda's bringing a helium tank, and we have Mylar balloons and sliver streamers. I think Betty and Marie are making a banner that says 'A Night in the Stars' or something like that."

When we got there, the place was buzzing with activity, and the second we walked in, a group of ladies rushed up to Mom with questions and concerns.

"Kathy, where should this go? Kathy, the tables aren't here yet. Kathy, should we order more ice? Kathy, the DJ needs to talk to you. . . ."

Mom was completely unflustered. Her eyes lit up, and she squared her shoulders. She handed me the box of Mylar balloons and started sorting through the questions. She walked across the gym with the gaggle of women behind her.

"Are those the balloons?"

"Yes."

"Come on over here, darling." Mrs. O'Connor waved me over to where Glenda stood with the helium tank on a dolly.

"Oh, good!" Glenda clapped. Mrs. O'Connor took the box from my hands, and the two ladies worked out a system.

"You fill and I'll tie. Samantha, can you hold them until we get a bunch ready to set around the gym?"

"Sure."

"You know, your mom was really smart to think of Mylar," Mrs. O'Connor said.

"Absolutely," Glenda agreed. "They won't deflate between now and tomorrow night."

They worked quickly, and I soon had fifteen balloons in each hand. They were surprisingly hard to hold and especially hard to walk with.

"Follow us," Mrs. O'Connor said, oblivious to the fact that my arms were beginning to shake. My palms were sweaty from gripping the silver strings so tightly.

"Let's put bunches of three along the bleacher railing up the stairs," Glenda suggested.

"Or we could start by putting them along the top railing every five feet or so."

"Okay, we just need to make sure we have enough to decorate at the entrance and for each of the tables."

"And I think it would be nice if the DJ had a bunch around his stand."

Beads of sweat broke out on my forehead. My hands cramped, and the strings began to slip. I gnashed my teeth together. "Please don't lose them now," I said to myself. "Maybe if I just . . ." I tried adjusting my grip, and in that second, thirty silver balloons floated up to the ceiling.

There was an audible gasp throughout the gym, and the moms stared at me, mouths agape.

Mom strode over. Now she was flustered.

"Did you just lose all of those balloons?"

"They were too hard to hold," I said, rubbing my throbbing, red hands.

Mom sighed irritably. "I brought you to help."

She glared at me and then looked at Glenda. "Is there enough helium if we get more balloons?"

"I think so."

"I'll make a balloon run," Mrs. O'Connor said.

"Thank you. Glenda, while she goes for balloons, we could use help with the streamers."

The two women walked over to the other end of the gym. I settled onto the bleachers and looked up at the ceiling. Except for the few balloons caught in the lights, I thought they looked good. Like stars, even, with shimmery tails.

"Don't worry," a lady sitting up a few rows from me said. "I think they make nice ceiling decorations." She winked and got back to her job of tying silver bows around bunches of blue carnations. I looked at the ceiling again, glad that someone saw it my way.

"They'll come down eventually," I overheard another lady reassure one of the assistant basketball coaches.

"Yeah, they will. During Monday's game," he huffed.

I hadn't thought about that.

Andy didn't get voted Homecoming King, but he was still excited.

"This is my last homecoming dance in high school," he said. That was how he was starting to think of everything. "This is my last first day of school in high school. . . . This is my last Halloween in high school. . . . These are my last high school pictures. . . ." He went on and on, and Evan thought it was obnoxious.

"You be sure to let us all know the last time you take a piss in high school," Evan said one morning. I thought Mom's eyes were going to pop right out of her head, and if the kitchen table hadn't provided a convenient barrier, she might have gotten her hands on Evan. He dashed out the door with a laugh, and Mom turned her attention to Daddy.

"Graham! Did you hear that?"

"What?" He looked up from his paper for the first time.

"Honestly," she shook her head.

"Don't worry, Mom. He's just jealous. Doesn't bother me. I'll be out of here soon enough."

I thought Evan's crack was pretty funny, but what Andy said was so final, like he couldn't wait to leave home, to get away from us. It made me feel like we were rushing into changes I wasn't ready for.

On the day of the dance, Andy spent hours washing and waxing his car. Then he went to work on the inside.

"Is the sweat smell gone?" he asked me when he was done. I hopped off the tire swing, where I had been watching him work, and gave his car a smell test.

"Not bad," I said. "Maybe Mom will let you spray some of her perfume in your car."

Andy wrinkled his face at this idea, but I thought it was the finishing touch his car needed. While he showered and got ready, Mom made a corsage with flowers from her garden. I watched her tie the bunch of pink and purple flowers with white ribbon. It was beautiful, and Mom looked so happy working on it.

When it was time for Andy to go pick up his date, Dad took a whole bunch of pictures of him in his light-blue tuxedo. Andy had so much aftershave on that I nearly choked when Mom made us pose for a picture together. My eyes watered, and I felt really sorry for his date. I almost suggested that he should drive with the windows down in hopes that he'd air out before he got there, but I decided to keep my ideas to myself. At least he wouldn't need that spray of Mom's perfume in his car.

Mom showed him how to pin the corsage to his date's dress, and I could tell that Andy was really nervous about poking her with the long, pearl-tipped pin.

Just before he headed out the door, he turned and asked if he could have a later curfew. "A group of us want to go to Denny's after the dance."

"Sure," Mom and Dad said at the same time. "You've earned it," Daddy said, and they sent Andy off to his last homecoming dance in high school.

Denny's? I guess I had a lot to learn about dates. I talked to Evan about this later that night, and he said he was pretty sure they weren't going to Denny's, but he wouldn't tell me where he thought they were going or what he thought they were doing. He said I was too young to know. I reminded him that I was almost thirteen, and he reminded me that I was twelve. End of discussion.

It was almost too cold to be sitting on Mrs. Brewster's porch, but the cups of cocoa helped. She was quiet for a long time after Evan told her that our mom had called him dumb. I didn't point out that Mom hadn't actually said the words. She didn't need to. It was obvious when she didn't say anything, and in a way, that was worse.

Mrs. Brewster sipped her cocoa and then lit up a big brown cigar. She puffed on it until it was going strong, and the little clouds of smoke floated over our heads. We knew she was ready to say something when she set her cigar to rest on her coaster. She licked her lips and picked a bit of tobacco from her tongue.

"Well, you have some choices to make. Why, you're nearly grown. Are you going to let words beat you down to nothing? If you don't like the way something's going, change it."

"He can't change moms," I said.

She laughed at this. "Of course not. That's not what I'm saying." She puffed some more and then dashed it out to save for later. "So, your mom said some mean things. You can stand up for yourself. I'll never understand why young people can't see that. Maybe you have to live fifty years."

For the first time I was mad at Mrs. Brewster. I felt like she was blaming Evan for the way things were. How could she tell him to just take a stand? It wasn't so simple, and isn't that what Mom and Dad were always saying? Make an effort. Try harder. The hot-chocolate taste soured in my mouth, and all of a sudden I blurted, "It's not his fault he can't read!"

"Samantha!" Evan yelled, and quick as lightning, he grabbed his bike and pedaled away.

I sat blinking, wishing I could take back what I had said. Mrs. Brewster put a heavy, calloused hand on mine.

I leaned forward, hoping Mrs. Brewster would say something that could fix everything. But she had nothing to offer, and my heart sank.

"I have to go," I said, fighting back tears. I could feel her eyes on me as I picked up my bike and rode away.

I was sure that Evan was in the woods, and despite the fact that the sun would soon set and rain clouds were rolling in, I was determined to find him.

Once I got to the woods, I had to walk my bike. The trees and shrubs became thicker and took over the rocky path I was following, and sure enough I came upon Evan's bike. I left my bike with his and trudged ahead. Then I spotted him.

"Samantha?"

"Evan!"

"I told you not to tell." He threw up his hands in frustration.

"I didn't think you meant Mrs. Brewster. We tell her everything."

"You promised! Don't you know what a promise is?" He shouted in my face, but I stood my ground.

"Why is it such a secret?"

"You don't understand, because you don't know what it's like."

Giant raindrops started to fall, but we ignored them.

"Tell me."

"Why? So you can run and tell everyone else?"

"You're the one who told Mrs. Brewster about what Mom said in the first place." He knew I had a good point.

The rain started to pour, but Evan continued. He leaned down so we were practically nose-to-nose. Little rivers of water ran down his face. And very slowly he said, "I . . . feel . . . stupid . . . every . . . day." His nostrils flared, and he was shaking.

"Things haven't always been this bad. How did you get this far?"

He broke into a sarcastic grin and shook his head. "They've always been this bad. Until now, Brian helped me a lot. He let me copy off of him and stuff like that. When we didn't have classes together in junior high, I just copied off of other people. You'd be amazed at how easy it is to get people to let me copy, like they just expect it. I even stole people's papers, erased their names, and put mine on them. That worked until I took the wrong girl's paper once."

"What do you mean?"

"Her handwriting was too good, and when the

teacher let her look through the stack of papers because she swore she'd turned hers in, she found it right away. My handwriting's so bad, they could tell that the paper wasn't mine. God, I hate that girl. She thinks she's perfect, and she just smirked the whole time Mrs. Freeman lectured me on how lazy and dishonest I was and that if I had just done my own work, I wouldn't be in trouble. I had to apologize to the whole class."

"I remember when you came home that day. Mom and Dad yelled at you for hours. But why haven't your teachers figured things out?"

"They have, Samantha. Mom and Dad think they're wrong about me. They never had any trouble with Andy, and they don't want to admit all their kids aren't perfect!"

"I'm not perfect," I said. This only brought a glare from Evan.

"Don't you dare."

I gulped and felt myself start to shake, and it wasn't because of the cold.

Evan slicked back his wet hair, and I became aware of the fact that I was soaked to the skin, but neither of us made a move to head for home.

"The funny thing is, I've noticed that every year my teachers figure me out pretty fast, and then they stop calling on me to read aloud. They don't ask me questions, either. It takes too damn long, and the rest of the class starts to get restless. That's why I hate having subs. When they call on me, the class groans."

He posed like he was reading a book. "S-S-Se-See . . . sp-spo-spot . . . rrrrun." He slammed the imaginary book shut and acted like he threw it over his shoulder. He turned away from me.

"I'll help you," I said, reaching out to him, but Evan laughed and flinched at my touch.

"Come on. It's dark, and we're soaked." He took my hand. "Mom's going to be pissed."

We walked, figuring there was no point in running, since we were already drenched. Evan grabbed both of our bikes and pushed them along.

"I really am sorry," I said.

"I know."

The butterflies that had begun to rage in my stomach as we got closer to home disappeared, especially when we saw that the only car in the driveway was Andy's. Evan parked my bike in the garage for me, and with water squishing out of our shoes every step of the way, we walked up to the front door.

"Where have you two been?" Andy opened the door and looked at us like we were crazy. We stood dripping and shivering.

"Got caught in the storm," Evan said. He moved toward the front door, but Andy blocked him.

"You can't come in like that."

Evan sighed and faced Andy. "Get us some towels, then," he demanded.

Andy closed the door on us, and Evan turned to me. "He's going to tell on us."

The butterflies came back to life as he kept us waiting on the porch for a good long time.

"Hurry up!" Evan yelled. Through the rippled panes of the side window, I could see a warped image of Andy taking his sweet time.

"Hold your horses," Andy said. He opened the front door and threw a towel at each of us. I wrapped up in it, slipped my shoes off, and started to make my way inside.

"Hold on there, squirt. What are you going to do for me to keep me from telling Mom and Dad you got home like a whole hour after dark?"

At exactly the same time, I said, "Dishes for a week," and Evan said, "Nothing." "Dishes for a week" was what Andy heard.

"Two weeks," he said as he folded his arms and stood square in the doorway.

All at the same time, I said, "Fine," Evan said, "No," and Andy said, "Deal," stepping aside to let us in. Evan shook his head. "You have a lot to learn about negotiating, Sam." I ignored him and went upstairs to get into dry clothes. Then I pushed my window open just enough to prop the Andy doll from my dollhouse on the ledge. I sent the doll flying out into the stormy night, hoping it landed in a deep mud puddle.

Chapter 10

I thought about what Evan had said about not being called on in class, and I realized that even in my class, there were those kids who just sat there all day. Some were troublemakers. A few went to work with a special teacher for part of the day, and then there were the sad ones. They looked pained and checked the clock a lot more than anyone else did. Their essays that were hung up on the wall among the others held little more than a few simple sentences. They never raised their hands, and Mrs. Teedle rarely called on them, and if she did, she asked them what I would call set-up questions and gushed with praise if they even came close to a right answer.

"Are you coming?" Gilbert asked when the bell rang for us to go home and I lingered at my desk.

"I'll catch up with you. I have to ask Mrs. Teedle something."

Gilbert looked confused. "I'll catch up," I said, waving him away and walking over to where Mrs. Teedle was erasing the board. A cloud of chalk dust billowed around her. I glanced up at the smiling face of President Reagan. When he'd been elected, every classroom had gotten a copy of his portrait to post next to the ones of Washington and Lincoln. I wondered what had happened to the pictures of Carter.

"Yes?" I looked up at her, and all of a sudden I was distracted by her hair. Was it a wig? Was Gilbert right? No. It couldn't be. Could it?

"Samantha?"

I forced myself not to look at her hair. "Just look at her eyes," I told myself, straining to focus. It was hard enough not to laugh at her orange polyester pantsuit. Mom would say that Mrs. Teedle was a woman in desperate need of a makeover.

"I know someone who can't read, and I wondered what kind of help that person could get."

"How old is he or she?"

"Older."

"Hmm. Well, that's a difficult situation. There are night classes at the community college in Lafayette. I think the high school even has an adult education program." She stopped and must have seen the disappointment in my face.

"What if the person isn't an adult yet? Do the parents have to give permission?"

"Samantha." She set aside a stack of papers and sat on the corner of a desk. "I know your brother Evan. He was a student of mine."

I was jolted. "I'm talking about someone else," I tried.

She cocked her head to one side and eyed me. "Yes. Parent consent is necessary until the person is eighteen. Parent consent is necessary for anything like testing for a learning disability, even if the teachers recommend it."

"I wish it wasn't," I said, and slung my backpack over my shoulder.

"You did the right thing by asking me about this. Your brother can get help. I know your parents are loving people, and they do care about Evan. . . ." She stopped like she was remembering something. "They would sit across from me in parent-teacher conferences and just wring their hands. One time we were all set to have him tested. Your parents were going to sign the permission forms. We'd explained everything to them about how once we had made our evaluations we could proceed with getting him the help he needs, more than the help I could offer in the classroom, and for some reason your mom refused at the last minute. Pen in hand, she just stopped and said no, and your father, I thought for a moment maybe he'd get her to change her mind." Mrs. Teedle shook her head. "My heart really goes out to them and Evan, and I can only imagine what it must be like for him in high school. The demands are so much greater, and I hate to say this, but the cracks for students to fall through are canyons in high school if they don't get the help they need before they reach . . ." She stopped suddenly like she realized she had said too much. Too late. No matter how hard I tried, I couldn't keep from crying. Mrs. Teedle handed me a tissue, and sure enough, she changed her tone. "Your parents are loving people. They'll find a way to get your brother the help he needs."

I blew my nose and wiped at my tears with the back of my hand. I managed a nod and headed for the door. Her parting words, "Talk to me anytime," trailed me as I left the room.

Gilbert was waiting for me by the flagpole.

"What's up?" He could see I had been crying. "Did you get into trouble?"

"Never mind. Do you want to get ice cream?"

"Naa. It's my day to go out with my dad. He's

picking me up at four o'clock, and he only has me until eight thirty-five on Wednesdays."

"Eight thirty-five?"

"No more. No less," he said. I could tell that he didn't want me to ask more about it. His parents had a strange way of working things out.

We walked along to his house, but when we got to the front steps, we were both struck by the sound of his mom yelling inside. Gilbert sighed and shook his head.

"What's going on?" I asked.

He didn't have to answer, because we could clearly hear what his mom was saying.

"It's your night to take him! You can't just cancel! I don't care what your girlfriend wants! I have a life, too!"

Like a balloon that suddenly lost its air, Gilbert crumpled on the brick steps. I sat next to him, but I didn't know what to say. It was like neither parent wanted him around for the night, and I thought that for the first time ever Gilbert wouldn't be able to smile his way through. His mom went on in a high-pitched, angry voice.

"Bill, we have a custody agreement. I am being reasonable!" There was a long pause, and all of a sudden Gilbert's mom was at the door. Her face was scrunched up so that her angry eyes squinted at us.

"Don't sit there eavesdropping! Gilbert, come inside. Samantha, go home!"

She didn't even have to finish what she was saying before my feet hit the street. I ran all the way home, where I was confronted by a driveway full of cars.

"What now?" I wondered out loud.

Inside Mom and her Women's Guild members were preparing posters and boxes for a canned-food drive for Thanksgiving. The smell of permanent markers was overwhelming, and I had to step over stacks of posters and boxes as I made my way inside. It took me a few moments to find Mom. She was sitting on the floor by the couch, decorating posters. I stood watching her for a while. She drew colorful designs and pictures on the posters inviting people to help the homeless by donating canned food.

"Hi, honey." She finally looked up and saw me. Her hair was pulled back, and she was dressed in her "work" clothes, a creased pair of jeans, navy Keds, and a floral-print dress shirt.

"Mom, guess what? I was over at Gilbert's and . . ."

"Can it wait? We have to get these posters done today. Then we have to take them downtown and put them in all of the local businesses." She gave me an air kiss and went back to decorating.

The only good thing about Mom hosting meetings was the table full of platters piled high with cookies, brownies, and lemon bars. I helped myself to one or two of each and slipped upstairs without being noticed.

"Hey, squirt!" Andy called out when I passed his room. I went back and stood in his doorway.

"Give me one of your cookies."

"Get some of your own," I said.

"Come on. I hate going down there. All those ladies ooh and aah over what a 'handsome young man' I am. They tell me about their nieces and daughters."

"Must be rough," I said, savoring one of my cookies. He gave me a pathetic look.

"Please?" He was sitting surrounded by piles of papers.

"What are you working on?" I went over to his desk.

"College applications. Now can I have a cookie?"

I looked at my plate. Somehow I'd managed to pick up an oatmeal raisin by mistake. It must have been mixed in with the chocolate chip cookies. Yuck.

"Here," I said, handing it to him.

"Thanks," he took it with one hand and then snatched a lemon bar off my plate with the other.

"Hey!" I yelled. "I'm telling! Mom! Mom!"

"Wait!" Andy shouted. "Here you go, you big baby." He split the lemon bar and gave half to me. I went out to the hall and looked down at Mom. She was standing with her hands on her hips, looking up at me angrily. I knew my complaint would fall on deaf ears.

"Never mind," I said quietly. I sat on the stairs and watched the ladies work.

One group wrote the information on the posters and passed them on to Mom's group, who decorated them and passed them on to a group who attached them to the sides of boxes that would be placed throughout Orinda, Lafayette, and the next town over, Moraga.

I liked watching Mom work. She seemed happiest when she had a project to complete. Every poster was a work of art when she was finished with it.

Just then Evan came in. He wound his way through the maze of boxes and posters and went straight for the goodies. He piled a plate much higher than mine and acknowledged the "handsome young man" comments with a quick, embarrassed grin before dashing upstairs.

"Hi." He smiled at me and told me to follow him to his room. He set his plate on his desk and unzipped his backpack. I watched him pull out a paper. Then he held it up for me to read.

I read aloud, "Lafayette Art Festival. November twenty-sixth through November twenty-eighth."

"It's an entry form. My teacher passed them out during homeroom." He pulled it away and turned his back to me. In a low voice he asked, "Can you . . . uh . . ." He faced me again and had such a pained look on his face, it broke my heart. "Can you help-me-fill-it-out?" He said it fast, as if he had to force himself and would not be able to ask again.

"Sure," I said, but for a moment Evan just sat there, and when he handed the form to me, he wouldn't look at me. I wanted to tell him that I was glad he asked me. That it was okay to ask me for help. But I was afraid to say anything that might upset him and make him change his mind.

He got up and pulled his chair out for me and flattened the form on his desk. I set my plate of goodies next to his and sat down. He handed me a brand-new pen, and of course it didn't work right away, so I had to scribble on a piece of scratch paper until the blue ink was rolling.

I looked at the form and saw that he had already filled in his name, but that was as far as he'd gotten.

"'Birth Date,'" I read aloud as I filled in the blanks. "'January 17, 1968. Age . . . Fourteen. Address . . . 137 Meadow Lane.'" I filled in our phone number, and then I wasn't sure about the next blank.

"It says 'Category,' and then it says, 'Amateur or Professional.' What's that?"

"I think I'm an amateur."

I checked that box.

"It says, 'Check One: Sketch, Oil Paint, Water-color, Photography, Mixed Media. . . . What's mixed media?"

"Mark 'Sketch,'" Evan said.

"'Title'? What do you call it?"

"Hmm. I haven't thought about that. Let's come back to that one."

"Okay. All you have to do is sign right here and . . ." Then I saw that if entrants were under eighteen, they needed parent consent.

"I wish you were eighteen! Parents have to sign right here."

He grinned, took the pen, and signed his name. Then he moved on to the next line and signed Daddy's name. He must have seen my concern.

"Don't sweat it. Entering an art contest isn't exactly a crime."

"Maybe you could just tell Dad about the art festival," I said.

"No way. If it's not about basketball or college, he's not interested."

He had a point.

"When does it say it's due?" Evan asked, biting into one of the three lemon bars on his plate.

I scanned the form. "It says the deadline is Friday, November nineteenth. It has to be hand delivered."

"You want to come with me? We can take the bus."

"Sure," I said as I polished off my second brownie.

We were quiet for a while as we worked our way through our plates of baked goods.

"My teacher said they give out prizes."

"What kind of prizes?"

Evan shrugged and offered me the oatmeal cookie he'd grabbed by mistake.

"Give it to Andy."

Chapter 11

The next day I met Gilbert by the flagpole in front of school. He was sitting hunched over, braiding and unbraiding the ties on his backpack. He didn't acknowledge me, but I sat down next to him anyway.

"Your dad didn't come for you, did he?"

He shook his head and hunched over more.

"That stinks."

The sun was still below the trees, so the cold air made me shiver. All of a sudden Gilbert sat up and looked around.

"What?" I asked.

"Let's ditch."

"What?" I asked again.

"Let's get out of here." He looked at me with a determination I had never seen before. He never did things like this. Just the thought of doing something against the rules gave him an asthma attack, but at the moment he was breathing deeply with his nostrils flared, and his eyes were angry.

I didn't say yes or no but started walking back through the parking lot, and sure enough Gilbert was right beside me. I figured that walking calmly was better than tearing out of there. We walked down a side street away from school, and when we were what we figured was a safe distance away, we stopped.

"So, what do we do now?" he asked.

"How am I supposed to know? This was your bright idea."

"Doesn't Evan ditch a lot?"

"He hasn't taught me how to!" I was exasperated.

Gilbert paced and muttered to himself, running through ideas of where we could go for the day. With each possibility that he tossed aside, his breathing became increasingly labored, until he stopped pacing and said, "Let's go back. I mean, what was I thinking? Come on. If we run, I bet we can make it and not even be late."

"Serious?"

He nodded emphatically and then broke into a run. I caught up with him, and the two of us were back at school in time for the first bell. Gilbert was out of breath, but his eyes were bright and he looked invigorated, maybe just at the thought of the adventure we almost had.

"Thanks, Sam," he said, and gave my hand a quick squeeze before he darted into the office where the school secretary had an inhaler for him to use in an emergency.

"Gilbert McNutt! What on earth?" I heard the secretary exclaim when she saw the state he was in.

"Move along, Miss Sheffield," Principal Gonzalez said on his way out to monitor the playground.

I told Evan all about our almost-adventure after school.

"You two are hilarious," he said, laughing as we walked home.

"I think Gilbert wanted to ditch because he's mad at his parents," I said.

"Probably." Then after a few steps he asked, "So, why did you go along?"

I thought for a moment. "Gilbert's my best friend and . . ." I was going to say that I was mad at our parents too, for the way they dealt with Evan, but I kept that to myself and was glad that he didn't ask me more about it.

Later that night in bed, I thought about it again.

I would have ditched the whole day if Gilbert had decided to, even though I knew that there was nothing that made our parents angrier than when Evan ditched school. Unable to sleep, I got out of bed and sat by my window for a while. Then on an impulse, I tiptoed to Evan's room. It took some effort to wake him.

"Let's go see the owls."

"Huh?" He squinted at me with sleepy eyes.

"The owls. Let's go see them."

He sat up and looked around. Then he got out of bed and listened for signs that anyone else was awake. Sometimes Andy stayed up late studying or doing push-ups in front of his closet mirror. I watched him once. He'd do a few push-ups and then check his muscles, posing like a bodybuilder. Sometimes I think guys are just as self-conscious about their looks as girls. I've even caught a glimpse of Gilbert checking out his muscles when he thought I wasn't looking.

When we were sure that the coast was clear, we made our way downstairs. We found our shoes, grabbed our jackets, and slipped outside. The chill in the air took my breath away for a moment, but the thrill of sneaking out and the possibility of seeing the owls drove away the cold.

We trudged to the same spot in the woods and

sat down on the crunchy blanket of pine needles. My pajamas weren't very good protection from the sharp needles, but I didn't care. I stared up at the clear night sky, heavy with twinkling stars, and waited.

I hardly blinked and had to remind myself to breathe. At any moment the owls could make their flight, and if I wasn't careful, I would miss it.

The wait grew long. Maybe we'd missed them. After all, if they only make that flight once a night, our chances of being there at exactly the right moment were pretty slim. I was about to ask Evan if he wanted to go back when I saw them. Against the black night, their white bodies glowed. They dipped and glided, soaring effortlessly. There was not a sound. And then they were gone.

I settled back and folded my arms in a pillow under my head. I didn't care about being cold, and I wasn't in a hurry to go inside.

All of a sudden, tears blurred my vision. Happy tears? Sad tears? It was hard to tell. I didn't want Evan to see me crying. And either he was sensitive enough not to ask, or he really didn't notice. After a while, he nudged me and said it was time to head home.

I was on my way to Mrs. Brewster's after school when Mom pulled up beside to me.

"Hop in," she said. I glanced down the road and back at our car. I saw that Evan was in the backseat and he did not look happy. With a nervous flutter, I got in.

"How was your day?" she asked. There was an edge to her voice.

"Fine," I said. I could taste the tension in the car.

"Hmm." Her lips were pressed together in a thin, angry line, and I swallowed nervously.

"Want to know what your brother did at school today?"

I slumped in my seat and leaned my head against the window. She was going to tell me, no matter what.

"He started a fire in science class! Fooling around and being careless as usual and got himself suspended for three days!" Her voice filled the car so that my eardrums hurt. I looked back at Evan, who had his arm out the window riding the wind current as if he didn't have a care in the world. But I knew that wasn't true.

"The whole school had to evacuate!" Mom yelled. Evan actually cracked a smile, which Mom caught in the rearview mirror, and I thought she was going to crash as she hit the gas and hardly slowed for the turn into our driveway.

"What are people supposed to do when there's a fire? At least I pulled the fire alarm!"

"You were messing around, not following directions!" she accused.

"Accidents happen!" Laughter bubbled up, and Mom whipped around in her seat.

"You shut your mouth!" she yelled. I screamed as the passenger side of the car grazed the hedges. Mom whipped back around and sped up our driveway, skidding to a stop and slamming the car into park.

"Go to your room! I don't even want to see your face!"

Evan got out of the car and walked toward the front steps. Mom was right behind him. My heart was pounding and my mouth was dry.

"Move it!" she yelled, shoving him in the back. Not expecting this, Evan tripped and fell against the steps.

"Don't!" I cried, but no one heard me because we were all distracted by Andy, whose car came roaring up the driveway.

"You jerk!" he yelled when he got out and stormed toward Mom and Evan. "I was a joke at practice today!"

Mom stood between the two with her arms out as if she could hold either one of them back. Andy towered over Mom, and Evan was at least a few inches taller than she was.

"You're such an idiot!"

"The fire was an accident!" Evan yelled. "How was I supposed to know that the stupid Bunsen burner would shoot a flame that high?"

"You're so stupid," Andy sneered. They moved toward each other. Mom waved her hands.

"You calm down," she said, pointing at Andy. Then she turned to Evan. "I told you! Go to your room! Now!"

When Evan didn't move right away, Mom started slapping at him. I burst into tears at the sight of Evan trying to shield himself as he stumbled up the steps backward.

"Don't! Mom, don't!" I cried, and rushed toward her, sobbing. Andy looked on with a scowl.

Evan got to the porch and ran inside. Mom stood on the steps, shaking with anger. Slowly, she lifted her eyes. "Don't be so dramatic." Andy went inside, and through the kitchen window, I could see him standing in front of the fridge, trying to decide on a snack.

All the while Mom and I just stood there. She moved toward me, but when I backed away, her shoulders fell. She pursed her lips, shook her head, and went inside, too. I turned and ran down the driveway.

I went straight to Mrs. Brewster's house. She was right where I hoped she'd be, and I sobbed out the whole story. She looked startled and confused, and again she had little more to offer than a sympathetic ear.

"My dear, this is hard to understand, but things won't change until Evan wants them to."

"I don't understand that! It's like you're saying it's his fault. He needs help!"

"Okay." She paused and sorted her words carefully. "Reckless behavior, forging signatures, and stealing apples are all cries for help, but they're the wrong cries. He needs to talk to your parents. They have to get to a point where they understand each other."

I leaned back against the soft cushions of the chair and watched Dudley make his way along the porch railing. He was nearly across when he lost his footing and landed in a bush with a sharp yowl.

Mrs. Brewster shook her head in amusement. "I don't think he knows he's a cat," she said.

"At least he landed on his feet," I said, checking to see if he was okay. With a flick of his tail, he ambled across the grass.

"He always does."

We were quiet for a while. My tears had dried, but I dreaded going home. I settled back and closed my eyes.

"Have you ever seen owls fly at night?" I asked, eyes still closed.

"I can't say that I have."

"I have. Twice. The timing has to be just right. Like seeing a rainbow. You have to be there at the right moment. It's really special, you know. More special than a sunrise or a sunset, because you know when that's going to happen."

"I'm sure it is," Mrs. Brewster said. I sat up and opened my eyes to look at her.

"You've seen rainbows, right?"

"A long time ago."

"It rains all the time here. All you have to do is pay attention."

A knowing smile spread over Mrs. Brewster's face.

"Don't you agree?"

"Sure." But she wasn't very convincing, and I felt confused.

"You're teasing me."

"Oh, honey, no. I'm not teasing you at all." She looked me in the eye.

A cold breeze swept across her porch, pushing dead leaves and ruffling the papers on her table.

"What, then?" I demanded.

"I think you're telling me about more than seeing owls and rainbows."

I didn't understand what she was saying.

"I'm talking about seeing owls. It's really amazing. Evan's making a picture of it."

"Good for him."

"Why are you being so . . ." I didn't know what the word was, but I didn't like feeling as if she knew something I should know that I was too dumb to figure out. "Stop teasing me!"

Mrs. Brewster's face flushed, and to my surprise, she reached across the table and clamped her hands on top of mine. I tried pulling free, but she only tightened her hold. There was no getting away until she decided to let go. I swallowed nervously and wondered what more she would say.

"You can't go away from here thinking that I would ever joke about something so important."

"Then tell me what you mean."

Her hold on my hands tightened.

"It was raining the day of the accident. I'll never forget the sounds. Pounding rain, squealing tires, clashing metal, my children crying. We spun off the road, and the car rolled over and over."

I did not want to hear this. I felt my throat tighten and made another useless attempt at pulling my hands free.

"We didn't wear seat belts in those days." She shook her head at the thought. "Stupid. Every one of us was thrown from the car. I blacked out, and when I came to, there was a deafening silence. The rain had stopped, and so had the crying of my children. I knew what that meant. A mother knows, but I was trapped, pinned under the car. All I could do was stare up at the sky, where the most amazing rainbow shimmered. All the colors were there in bold bands from end to end, and then it grew pale, became see-through, and finally faded away.

"Afterward, I kept asking people, the paramedics, doctors, nurses, if they'd seen the rainbow. They thought I was hallucinating. It was understandable, though, and they patted my hands and gave me sympathetic looks and more painkillers."

For more than two years I had wondered about the accident, and not once could I have imagined how bad it really was. She let go of my hands, but I was too numb to move.

"I've never told anyone this."

"I'm sorry." I wasn't sure if I'd said it out loud. If I hadn't, I decided I wouldn't repeat it, because "I'm sorry" was a ridiculous thing to say. After all that, "I'm sorry" didn't even begin to touch what I wanted to say to her.

"You'd better get home." She released the brakes on her wheelchair and headed for her front door.

"Go on," she said as she pushed her door open. It took her a couple of tries to get over the threshold. Once she was in, she closed the door behind her, and I headed for home.

Chapter 12

I walked slowly. The sun had set long ago, but I didn't care.

Daddy was home, and as I walked up the steps I wasn't surprised at the sound of Mom and Dad yelling. But they weren't in the living room or the kitchen as I had expected. Andy was sitting at the kitchen table, and I was struck by the solemn look on his face. He glanced at me with worried eyes.

Then Evan's cry made me shudder. I stood against the front door and looked up at his room. Shadows on his ceiling moved about in some kind of struggle. The shadows moved faster, and Evan cried again.

"Don't touch that! You can't take that! It's mine!" His voice broke.

Mom came out of his room carrying a huge stack

of his artwork. She stormed down to the kitchen and out to the garage with it. Was she throwing it away? I stood frozen, wondering what was next. She went back up to his room again and came out with his art case. I don't think she even saw me in her fit of rage.

She took the case to the garage too, but my attention was drawn to Evan's room, where Daddy had a hammer and screwdriver.

"No more, Evan!" Daddy yelled, and hammered the screwdriver against the hinges on his door. "No more slamming the door and shutting us out!" It took Daddy only a moment to take Evan's door off the hinges, and then it was his turn to make a trip to the garage. I couldn't believe what I was seeing.

On his way back inside, he did a double take when he caught a glimpse of me sitting on the floor by the front door. He stepped over and squatted down in front of me. He looked like he was on the verge of crying and gently cupped my face.

"At least give him his art back," I whispered. His face flushed, and his eyes did fill with tears as he slowly shook his head.

"You don't understand," I said, pulling his hands away from my face. He cleared his throat and made his tears go away before they could fall. He got up and looked toward Evan's room. Mom was still up there. I could hear her voice but couldn't make out what she was saying.

Finally, she came out with a red face, her mouth pinched, arms folded. She had to know this was wrong. What they were doing was wrong. She avoided our looks and moved slowly, stiffly down the hall to their room. Then the house was silent and still in a frightening kind of way that made me cold deep inside.

"Daddy, how can you do this?" I got to my feet.

"Stop," he said in a weak voice, and started to walk into the kitchen.

"Why do you always go along with Mom?"

At this he whipped around and glared at me. I could see his jaw muscles twitching.

"Go to your room," he said through clenched teeth.

I threw up my hands. "That's your answer for everything!" I had never dared to speak to him like this, and I wondered if he could see that I was trembling.

"Go," he said in a deep voice, straining to keep control. But I had gone too far to stop now.

"Look at our family! Do something! Help Evan instead of hurting him!"

I saw Andy shake his head. He got up and went outside. Daddy looked at the closing door and back at me.

"All you care about is work, and your stupid birdhouses, and Andy's score in basketball!" I screamed at the top of my lungs. At this Daddy raised his hand to slap my face, I ducked, and he got control of himself. The effort made him shake, and he didn't have to tell me again. I scrambled to my feet and ran upstairs to my room.

I fell onto my bed and stared at the ceiling. At the faint buzz of Daddy's power saw and the whir of his drill, I slammed my window shut and paced angrily, stopping once when I heard the engine of a car. Andy had the luxury of escaping, and I envied him. I sat on the floor and pulled out the bottom drawer of my dresser. I sifted through old birthday cards, rocks, seashells, and flowers dried to the point that they crumbled into a brown powder when I touched them. I ran my hands over photos from happier times, found one of my baby teeth tucked in the back corner of the drawer, and then I got to what I was looking for—pictures Evan had drawn for me. I looked through the stack and regretted that the edges of a few were curled. Carefully, I smoothed them as best I could. Then I returned them to their special place and stretched out on the floor.

When I woke the house was quiet. Mom and Dad were sleeping. I went to Evan's room. He was curled up on his bed, still dressed; I thought he was asleep.

"I heard what you said to Dad," he said. I was startled at first, then glad. He sat up and made room for me to sit next to him. "They took everything. They even took the goddamn door." He half laughed and half cried at the absurdity of it.

"What if we could get your artwork back?" I asked.

"What do you mean?"

"I saw Mom take it to the garage."

"She probably trashed it."

"Let's get it out of the trash."

"Forget it. They'll see that we did that."

"The trash goes out in the morning. They won't check, and we'll hide it."

Evan lay back down and curled up again. My heart sank, but I wasn't going to give up. I headed for the kitchen, sure that Evan would come along, but he didn't.

The door to the garage made a loud creaking noise so I opened it very slowly, just enough to slip into the garage. I was surprised at how cold the concrete floor was on my bare feet and reached up for the chain to turn on the light, but even on tiptoe, I couldn't reach it.

"Shoot," I muttered in the pitch dark. I reached

for the doorknob to go back for a flashlight, and just when I grabbed it, someone pulled the door open and I fell into the kitchen. Sure that I had been caught, I stifled a surprised cry. When I saw that it was Evan, I breathed a sigh of relief. We moved back into the garage, and as soon as the door was closed, Evan reached up for the chain.

One by one we lifted the lids and peered into each of the four green trash cans. No artwork, but plenty of stink. Evan even pulled out the sacks that nearly filled each can, though we were both sure that his drawings would have been at the top if they were in the cans.

"Maybe she just hid them somewhere," I said. I liked the idea that maybe Mom couldn't actually bear the thought of throwing his artwork away. We started searching the garage. Boxes were stacked from floor to ceiling. They were taped closed, so we knew that there was no point in looking inside. One whole wall of the garage was Daddy's workbench, and it was clean, except for a bit of sawdust and his works in progress. We each took a sidewall and peered into the nooks and crannies of what space wasn't filled with boxes or sports equipment.

"I don't get it. I saw her come out here with them. She came back empty-handed."

"My art case too?"

I nodded. Forlorn, Evan sat on a crate beside Daddy's workbench and buried his face in his hands. His bedroom door was propped beside him.

"I wanted to enter that art festival more than anything. I was going to call my sketch *Flight*."

"Can you make another picture?"

He looked at me like I was crazy. The deadline to enter was just two days away. "I give up," he said as he stood and turned out the light. Long past cold, my feet had begun to ache. I followed him back inside, and as we tiptoed past Mom and Dad's room, we froze at the sound of them talking. Their voices weren't much more than a whisper.

"I'm just not sure throwing his artwork out was the right thing to do," Daddy said.

"He needs to be punished," Mom said, and Evan started to move on, but I stayed put. I wanted to hear more.

"He's artistic, like you are," Daddy said. "You enjoy doing crafts. Did you really look at some of his drawings? He's talented."

I looked to Evan, who had stopped again. I couldn't see for sure, but I figured he was holding his breath. He moved back toward their door.

"He is talented, but where will that get him? It's like you said, he doesn't have the drop-out option."

There she went again. I thought back to the last time I'd overheard them talking. Why did she always bring up her own years in high school?

"Kathy, this isn't about your options. What options are we going to give him?" Daddy's voice was heavy and met only by silence.

Evan and I stood in the hall long after they'd stopped talking. Finally, we gave up and went to my room. We sat on my bed, not looking at each other for what seemed like ages. Then I blurted it out, the question that had been on my mind for days, "Did Mom graduate from high school?"

Evan looked at me then. "Do the math, Sam. Andy came before any diploma." He stood up and gave me a sad smile. "Don't worry about it. Get some sleep."

Chapter 13

The next morning was cold and foggy, which was perfect, because that's exactly what our house felt like. We ate in silence, and when I was finished with my Froot Loops, Mom told me to get going.

I had more than enough time, but I didn't argue. I was glad to get away from all the tension. I walked by the trash cans that had been pulled out by my father earlier that morning and felt a flutter of nerves at the sound of the approaching garbage truck.

"It's not in there," I told myself. "We checked." But that didn't make me feel any better as the trash collectors in their blue coveralls hopped down, flung the lids off the cans, and dumped them. I watched for a moment and then turned and ran all the way to school.

On the playground I saw Gilbert, casually slung between the two parallel bars.

"You want to go to B&B today?" he asked.

"I'm broke," I said, settling onto the bars.

"My treat," he said with a smile.

"Great."

We did go to B&B, and this time Gilbert bought five licorice ropes and two King Size Milky Ways. He bought me one of those lollipop rings that looks like a giant diamond. It was a choice between grape flavor or sour apple, and I went for grape.

"Good choice," Gilbert said.

"So how many licks did it take to get to the center of your jawbreaker?" I asked on our way home.

"More than three hundred and twelve. My mom found it in my sock drawer and threw it away before I got to the middle."

"Too bad."

"I'll try again sometime," he said with his licorice ropes draped around his neck.

When I got home, no one was there, and I figured Mom had made Evan go with her on her errands. As I made my way past Andy's room, something caught my eye. I stopped in the hallway and turned back to his room.

"Is that what I think it is?" I asked myself, daring to enter Andy's room, which was a big no-no unless he granted permission.

Sure enough, the edges of Evan's artwork were sticking out from under Andy's dresser. I fell to my knees and carefully pulled out the stash. Why was it here?

Frantically, I looked through the stack until I came to *Flight,* the sketch Evan wanted to enter in the art festival. I sat back in a moment of happy relief and looked at the clock beside Andy's bed. It was four o'clock. That's when I caught sight of Evan's art case. This was too good to be true.

I gathered up his artwork and case and took it all to my room. I did a better job of hiding the other pieces than Andy had, tucked the art case deep in the back of my closet, and gently rolled up *Flight.* I stopped by Evan's room and found the entry form we had filled out. "I can't believe it!" I smiled to myself, looking over the form. I got two steps into the hall and ran right into Andy. Stunned, I dropped the sketch and the entry form. I looked up at Andy's angry face. "What were you doing in my room?"

"Why did you take Evan's artwork?" I asked.

His face softened. "I just didn't think it should be thrown away."

We locked eyes for a moment, and then I gathered up the sketch, hoping he wouldn't press me about going into his room. He shrugged and moved past me.

"I came home to get a few things to work on at the library. Tell Mom I'll be there for a while. I've got a project to finish," he called from his room.

In a moment he came out with a bulging book bag slung over his shoulder. "Never mind. I'll leave her a note."

"I can remember to tell her."

He just grinned and hurried downstairs, where he dashed a quick note and stuck it to the fridge with a magnet before rushing out the front door. I tucked the entry form into my back pocket, and in the kitchen junk drawer I found a rubber band to secure the sketch. Then I set it in the basket of my bike so it would be out of sight and ready to go.

I paced by the front door, and with each tick of the grandfather clock, I felt my nerves tighten. We had to get to the depot by four thirty to make the bus to Lafayette, and it was almost four fifteen. Just then I caught a glimpse of Mom's car and ran to the front door. Mom saw my excited face and smiled brightly. I guess she thought I was happy to see her. I felt a pinch in my heart, because the truth was I wasn't happy to see Mom at all.

Like a ghost, Evan slipped inside. I started to go after him, but Mom called me.

"Hi, honey! Come help me grab these bags. Just wait until you see what I got for the centerpieces at the mission on Thanksgiving."

I hesitated. "Samantha." Her smile turned to a look of disappointment. I walked over to her car, and she handed me two sacks of fake fall leaves. She carried a sack of twigs and acorns. I followed her inside and set the bags on the kitchen table.

"Mom, I have to go to Gilbert's to work on a project."

"Oh. I thought maybe we could work together on these centerpieces. You know, a little mother-daughter time." She looked at me with such hopeful eyes.

Lying to her was harder than I thought it would be, and there was a part of me that wanted to jump at a chance for a little mother-daughter time. But my heart was set, and I steeled myself against backing down.

"The project's due tomorrow," I said, looking at the floor, avoiding the disappointment in her face.

"Okay."

My breath caught in my throat when she stepped out to the garage. I was sure she'd see the sketch in my basket. But she came back in humming happily as she plugged in her glue gun and set out her other craft tools.

"Aren't you going to Gilbert's?" she asked.

"Yeah. I just have to get a few things from upstairs."

Evan was sitting at his desk.

"Evan," I whispered. He looked at me with dull eyes. "Your sketch is in the garage right now. If we hurry, we can make it to the community center and turn it in."

There was a flash of excitement in his face that flickered and went out.

"Sure, I'll just stroll on down and let Mom know," he said, shaking his head.

"You can sneak out your window."

"I don't have a door, remember? She'll notice I'm gone."

"She's busy making leaf things for the soup kitchen. We can get there and back before she ever notices."

The light came back to his face as he looked at his bedroom window and then peered out into the hall. We could both hear her humming.

"Close the window after me."

"Yes!"

The smell of the glue gun stung my nose as I made my way through the kitchen to the garage to get my bike. Mom didn't even look up from her work of sorting out the orange, yellow, and red leaves.

"Bye," I called.

"Bye, honey."

Evan was already in the garage when I got there, and in the blink of an eye the two of us were sailing down the driveway. We decided it would be safer if I rode on the handlebars of his bike and held on to the sketch. Perched on the handlebars, I strained to hold on to the sketch without crushing it. Evan pedaled so fast that the trees and shrubs along the side of the road were a green blur. The cold air made my eyes sting, but I was too afraid to shut them, so I squinted and braced myself as best I could.

We made it to the depot and locked his bike in the bike rack.

Evan paid our way, and, just to be sure, he asked, "This bus goes to the Lafayette Community Center, right?" The driver managed a slight nod, and we took the seats nearest the door. Evan was smiling, the sweat dripping down his face.

"That was a wild ride," I said now that I could stop and think about it. Evan laughed.

We sat in quiet agony every time the bus made a

stop along the way. I began to feel like we were never going to get there. Evan must have felt the same way. Long before our stop, he stood gripping the metal rail and peering out the windshield.

"The entry form! We forgot the entry form!"

"It's right here." I pulled it out of my pocket, and he took it and slipped it into his back pocket.

Finally the bus rolled to a stop in front of the community center. We bounded down the steps and ran inside.

"Where's the art festival?" Evan asked a lady who was seated at a reception desk.

"Down the hall, first door on the right."

"Thanks," we said.

"Hold on a moment," the lady said. We stopped in our tracks and looked back at the tall, pointy-nosed lady.

"Is that an entry?" she asked, pointing to the roll I was still holding. Sure she wanted to admire Evan's work, I started to slide the rubber band off.

"Yeah," Evan said. "It's mine."

He pulled the entry form from his back pocket.

"Where's the frame?"

"What?" Evan asked. Snap! The rubber band broke and landed somewhere behind her desk. The lady flinched.

"What do you mean?" Evan asked.

The lady sighed and pulled out a blank entry form. She drew a yellow marker over the small print and then read the words to us.

"All entries must be mounted or framed, ready to hang."

I snatched the entry form out of Evan's hand and read the same line. How did I miss that?

"Where do I get a frame?" Evan asked.

"There's a shop down on Main Street. Oh, but it closes at five o'clock."

"Can't you make an exception?" I asked.

She laughed softly, and I felt my face get hot. A lump grew in my throat as she shook her head. I glanced down the hall. Stacks of entries were propped along the walls ready to be displayed—all framed.

"Come on," Evan said.

I followed him across the street to the bus shelter. It was dark, and I wondered if my lie about going to Gilbert's was holding up okay. Neither of us spoke, and when the bus arrived, we boarded and went all the way to the back. I stared out the window, but the lights inside the bus made it so that I could see only my reflection. I could see Evan slouched in his seat, staring at the floor.

I unrolled *Flight* and stared at it. Every time I looked at his sketches, I noticed different details. This time I noticed how he'd made the owls' feathers look soft yet sleek. I saw the intricate detail he put into drawing their claws, tucked in for the flight, ready to clutch their prey in an instant.

Then the driver turned off the lights, and I couldn't see a thing. Evan hunched over and swiveled away from me with his arms wrapped around himself.

"We can get a frame somewhere," I said. "The deadline isn't until tomorrow night." Then it hit me. Nearly every wall in Mrs. Brewster's house was covered with framed pictures—paintings, prints, and photographs of all sizes.

"We can go to Mrs. Brewster's."

"She's in the frame business?" he asked with his back to me.

"You've seen her walls. I know she'd let you take one of her pictures out and put yours in."

He considered for a moment as I gently rolled the sketch again.

"That might work," he said, swiveling around.

"I know it will. We've gone this far. We can't give up now and we may not be able to sneak away again tomorrow."

When the bus pulled into the Orinda Depot, he asked the driver if there was another bus to Lafayette that night. The driver's answer was a bus schedule. Evan grimaced.

"Can't you just tell me?"

"I make my final run to Lafayette at six thirty."

"What time is it now?" Evan pushed his luck.

"Time for you to get a watch," the driver said, nodding toward the clock tower in the middle of the depot.

"Five forty-five," I called, leaping down the steps and dashing over to Evan's bike. Nervously, Evan struggled with the lock. Finally, he freed his bike. Then it was another wild ride—even wilder in the cold black night. With every breath, I inhaled the smoky scent of fireplaces mixed with the earthy pine-needle smell of yards still wet from the last rain.

When we got to Mrs. Brewster's, we ran up to her porch and knocked on the door. It seemed like it took her hours to answer.

"Who is it?" she asked in a voice anxious at unexpected visitors.

"Evan and Samantha!"

"Oh! Hold on!" We could hear her situating her wheelchair so she could unlock the door and pull it open.

"To what do I owe this visit?" she asked with a bright smile.

Out of breath and in a rush, we explained. Her eyes lit up with anger when we told her about how Mom had thrown Evan's artwork away. She pushed her eyebrows together like she was trying to solve a really hard math problem, one of those word problems. She must have wondered how a mom could be so hard on her son.

Evan looked at the floor. His hair was damp with sweat, and he struggled to slow his breathing as he recovered from our ride.

"We have to hurry," she said, glancing at the clock.

Evan took his sketch and unrolled it. Mrs. Brewster did a double take and then just stared.

"This is incredible," she said, emphasizing each word. "You are truly talented."

Evan smiled shyly.

"Let's see, it looks to be about sixteen by twenty." She scanned her walls. "That one. Get that one. It's the right size and color." She pointed at the framed photograph hanging over the fireplace. It was a picture of the beach on a stormy day. I was struck by the fact that there was not one single picture of her family anywhere. My eyes darted from one photo or painting to another, all scenes of nature. They were the kind of pictures you'd see in a doctor's office or at a hair salon—impersonal. Safe.

"Pull that chair over and climb up there."

Evan did as she said.

"Good. Now let's take it to the kitchen table." She led the way. "Turn it over. See those clips?" She told Evan how to take the frame apart, and when he slipped the photo out, she took it and set it aside. Evan's sketch was a perfect fit, and in seconds we had the clips and the wire back in place. *Flight* was ready for hanging, looking even better in the dark frame with gray-blue matting.

"Six fifteen. You've got to be on your way! Go on now." Mrs. Brewster rolled down the hall to the front door.

"Thank you," we said. Before I got out the door, Mrs. Brewster grabbed my hand and pulled me down to her. She said nothing but looked me in the eyes and nodded. When I started to look away, she squeezed my hand to get my attention again. I wasn't sure I understood what she was trying to communicate and didn't get a chance to ask.

"Hurry up!" Evan called.

It was even harder to perch on the handlebars and hold the framed sketch. We had a few false starts until we figured it was better for me to sit on the seat, holding the frame between us. Evan pedaled standing up the whole way, and I was able to clutch his shirttails with one hand and hug the frame to my body with my other arm.

Luck was in our favor, because we made it to the depot again just as the driver was ready to make his final run for the day. We paid and sat in the front seats. The only other person on the bus was the guy who took our order at Nation Burger. He didn't recognize us, but I knew him: Pimple—and his complexion was not getting better.

He sat in the middle section of the bus, eyes closed, head against the window. I figured he must have taken this route often, because he was undisturbed by the bumps and bounces, and at just the right time, he opened his eyes and moved to the exit. I watched him get off and go into a market. Every light post in the parking lot of the market was decorated with red-and-white tinsel candy canes, and the sliding doors had painted scenes of snowdrifts and elves. I think they had been that way since the day after Halloween, which made Mom mad. She believed that no Christmas decorating should be done before Thanksgiving.

"He works two jobs," Evan said, acknowledging the fact that I was watching Pimple.

"Really?"

"Ever since his dad took off, he's been helping his mom out. He's got a whole bunch of little brothers and sisters. The kids at school tease him all the time."

My stomach clenched, and I vowed never to think of him as Pimple again.

"His name's Mike," Evan said as if he could read my mind.

It was six forty-five when we got to the Community Center, and I could see how surprised the lady at the reception desk was when we walked in. She smiled and pointed us down the hall.

"Ah! Another entry!" a very excited man said when we got to the end of the hall. "Amateur?"

"Yeah."

"Excellent." The man took Evan's sketch and entry form.

"Is that it?" Evan asked.

"Uh-huh. We'll see you next week."

We headed down the hall but froze when the man called out, "Hold on!"

"What now?" I wondered out loud.

"Is this sketch untitled? You don't have anything where it says title."

"Oh." Evan took the form and the pen the man

offered, but that was as far as he got. He couldn't read on the form where to write *Flight,* and I could tell that he was embarrassed. I pulled Evan to the floor. Crouched over the form, I pointed to the line and spelled out *F-l-i-g-h-t.*

"Excellent," the man said, taking the form and tearing the bottom portion off. He taped this to the back of the frame and filed the top half. Then he added Evan's sketch to one of the many stacks.

Outside was cold enough to see our breath, and I wished I had thought to grab a heavy jacket. The street was quiet and grew even quieter as the minutes passed. I began to shiver.

"Here it comes," Evan said, stepping off the curb and peering at the first pair of headlights we'd seen in a solid twenty minutes.

"Finally." I joined Evan in looking at the approaching headlights.

"Ev, that's . . ." I grabbed his arm and didn't have to say anything more.

"It's just a truck!" Evan exclaimed, stomping his foot.

"Do you still have that schedule?"

Evan pulled it out of his back pocket and handed it to me.

"What number was the bus we took?"

"How should I know?"

I scanned the rows and columns of times, bus numbers, and abbreviated destinations. Then my eyes landed on an asterisk. I read the message to myself first, and my shivers turned into trembles.

"What?" Evan asked. "What's it say?"

"Final runs to Lafayette do not return to Orinda! We're stuck here!"

It took a moment for what I said to register with Evan. Slowly he closed his eyes and groaned. "We have to call Mom," he said.

My legs felt weak, and I forgot about being cold. "There has to be some other way," I said, but I knew better. Once again we approached the lady at the reception desk. "Can we borrow a phone?" Evan asked.

"Sure." The lady slid her phone across the counter. "Dial a nine first."

"You do it," Evan said to me.

"No. You."

"No way."

"You have to," I said.

"Why?"

"You're older."

Evan cracked up and shoved the receiver my way. I refused to take it. He dialed, and I held strong, pressing my lips together. I could hear the phone ringing and then, "Hello?" Mom's voice.

"Talk to her!" Evan whispered, pushing the phone at me.

"You!" I pushed it back.

"Hello? Who is this?" Mom's voice came again, and then the line went dead.

"Ugh!" Evan groaned. "I can't believe you!" He hung up and dialed again. This time he didn't try to get me to talk. I was distracted by the receptionist, who was watching us with great curiosity. I offered no explanation.

"Mom?" He got one word in before she went ballistic. Evan could actually hold the phone a foot away and we could both hear everything she said. Every once in a while, he tried to talk to her.

"Mom . . . I . . . we . . ." It was impossible. All of a sudden, he set the receiver on the counter and walked out the door.

The receptionist and I looked at each other. The high-pitched, frantic chatter was still pouring from the phone. I had no choice but to pick up where Evan left off.

"Mom."

"Samantha? I called Gilbert! You're not there! You never were there!"

"I know, but you don't have to be worried."

"Where are you?"

"The Lafayette Community Center," I said, and the phone went dead.

I hung up and pushed the phone back across the counter. "Thank you," I said, then walked out to the parking lot, where Evan was waiting.

"She's on her way, I think."

"What do you mean, you think?"

"I told her where we are and she hung up."

"She's coming."

We sat down on the curb and waited. Somehow I wasn't upset. I knew I'd probably be grounded and for sure I'd have to listen to lots of yelling, but it was okay. It was worth it. I glanced back at the community center, where a banner was slung between two pillars, and read out loud, "'Fifteenth Annual Amateur'—that's you—'and Professional'—you someday—'Art Festival. November twenty-sixth to November twenty-eighth.'"

We shared smiles, and, crazy as it seemed, I felt happy.

Chapter 14

Soon enough, Mom came tearing into the parking lot, and my hold on happiness slipped a bit. She hopped out and stormed over to us.

"What's going on?" she demanded. She looked behind us at the quiet community center, and I thought she'd see the banner and figure things out.

"Well?" She looked at each of us and then turned her attention to me. "Samantha, I will not have you start taking after your brother!"

"Which one?" I sassed, and Mom slapped my face.

"Whoa!" Evan cried.

She was a lot quicker than Daddy, and the sting on my cold cheek really hurt.

"Don't get smart," she said. I covered my cheek

with my hand and looked up at her. She pointed a finger in my face and demanded an explanation. I gulped and continued staring at her. She raised her hand again, and I squeezed my eyes shut, bracing myself, but another slap never came.

"Kathy?" At a woman's voice from behind me, I opened my eyes, and Mom's face slipped from anger into pleasant surprise. It was frightening to hear her voice go from stone cold to joyful as she greeted her acquaintance.

"Sylvia! How are you?" Mom moved around us and approached the lady. I didn't recognize her and glanced at Evan, who shrugged and put an arm around my shoulders. "I'm sorry," he whispered.

"I'm not."

The two women hugged and started chatting away. Sylvia had obviously not seen Mom hit me. Or was she just as good at acting like nothing was wrong?

"Are you still with the Senior Citizen Center here?" Mom asked.

"Oh, yes. It's so rewarding. We're getting ready for our Thanksgiving event."

"Wonderful," Mom enthused.

"Is that . . . ?" The woman looked past Mom at us. "It can't be. The last time I saw Evan and Samantha, they were this high!" She held her hand near the ground and laughed.

"Those are my two youngest. And can you believe our Andy is applying to college? We're sure he's going to get a basketball scholarship. Of course, he's doing so well academically, he could just as easily earn an academic scholarship. They grow up so fast." I could hear the strain in Mom's voice as she worked to sound as if all was well.

"Say hello," she commanded, widening her eyes at us.

"Hi," I managed, but Evan stayed silent.

"Your mom is a real powerhouse," Sylvia said. My cheek throbbed.

"Oh, Sylvia. You're too kind," Mom said with a flourish. "Listen, it looks like you've got your hands full," Mom said, acknowledging the cart full of paper goods and decorations. "I've got to run, too. I'm in the middle of making centerpieces for our Thanksgiving dinner at the mission this year. Busy, busy! Bye, now." She waved and smiled until Sylvia was on her way inside. Then her smile vanished. "Get in," she snapped.

Evan and I climbed into the backseat, and I was glad for the warmth, no matter how bad things were.

"This is my fault. You don't have to be mad at Sam," Evan tried.

"You lied to me!" She ignored Evan. "Do you have any idea how embarrassing it was to call Gilbert's house? I looked like a fool!"

"I'm sorry," I said in a small voice. Was she more upset about being embarrassed or not knowing where we were? The question made me even more sure that what we had done was right.

"I want an explanation!"

"I don't have one," I said.

Mom threw up her hands. I was beginning to realize that she should not drive when she's angry. In her rage she drove through a stop sign and nearly missed our driveway. When she came to a stop, the three of us sat in the car for a moment.

"Of course . . ." Her voice cracked. "Your father is still at work . . . when I need him most." She squeezed the steering wheel until her knuckles turned white.

"Evan, go to your room. Samantha, you are going to sit in the kitchen until your father gets home. Maybe he can get an explanation out of you."

I gulped nervously. Evan walked up to his room. For once, I wished that she'd just send me to my room.

Inside, she pulled out a kitchen chair for me, and

I took a seat. She busied herself with cleaning up, haphazardly throwing scraps of leaves and twigs into a box. A few acorns rolled and dropped onto the floor. I started to go for them, but Mom stopped me.

"Sit. I'll get them." She crouched down and searched. She didn't see the one by the sink until she stepped on it and cursed angrily, bending down to snatch it up and add it to the box of leftovers. She was the kind of angry that made her clumsy and mad at me for things that weren't really my fault.

"The centerpieces are pretty," I said, acknowledging the ten arrangements of leaves, twigs, and acorns that sat on the table. It looked like there was a place for a large candle in the middle of each one.

Mom eyed me and checked to see if the glue gun was cool enough put away, swept the scraps from the counter into the box, and took it out to the garage. She came back with two empty boxes and carefully stacked five centerpieces in each one.

Next she pulled out a package of hamburger meat. She dunked the meat into a bowl and proceeded to make meat loaf. It was one of her better dishes, and my stomach was roaring.

"I love meat loaf." Her only reply was another cold look. Then she glanced at the clock and clicked her tongue.

"Where is Andrew?"

"He's at the library. There's the note he left you right there," I said, pointing to the refrigerator.

Mom scoffed and yanked the note from under the magnet. She balled it up and threw it in the trash. "You could have told me sooner."

My jaw dropped. She was going to blame me for everything. She went to work on a head of lettuce, chopping and tossing it and other salad makings into a large blue salad bowl. The smells of dinner were making my mouth water, and I got up to set the table in hopes that we would eat soon.

"What do you think you're doing?"

"Setting the table?"

"Sit."

I flopped back into my chair in torture. "Mom, we didn't do anything bad."

"Stop! Save it for your father."

And as if on cue, his headlights lit up the front yard. He got one foot in the door, and Mom whisked him upstairs to their room. It didn't take her long to fill him in, and soon Daddy confronted me. He had taken off his tie and loosened his collar.

I looked up at my father's tired eyes. He had his arms folded, and there was a definite five o'clock shadow on his face.

"What in the world were you doing traipsing about behind your mother's back? Since when is it okay for you to lie?"

"We had to take care of something, and I can't tell you . . ."

The look of astonishment on my father's face was almost more than I could take.

". . . for now," I added quickly. "I can't tell you for now."

"Samantha Leigh! You tell your father what you were doing right now!"

"No," I said, surprised at myself.

Mom's face turned red, and her eyes were so wide I could see the whites all the way around. She made a move toward me, and I put my hands up to protect myself. Daddy grabbed her.

"Okay. Okay." He put an arm around her. "Honey, calm down. No one got hurt, and we're not going to spend the whole night trying to get an explanation out of her."

Mom turned and put her hands on Daddy's chest. "You don't know how awful it was, Graham." She was in tears, and Daddy looked past her at me with anger and disgust. He hugged Mom and rubbed her back.

"Kathy, let's get dinner on the table. It smells

delicious. We all need a hot meal and a moment to catch our breath." Then to me, "Set the table."

I did as he told me to, including a place for Andy because Mom was sure he'd be home any moment. Daddy called Evan to the table, and for the umpteenth time he told Mom how delicious everything looked and smelled, and that the centerpieces were her best yet.

I was on pins and needles waiting for Mom to snap again and tried to be as invisible as possible. I could see Evan trying to read the situation as he took his place at the table. Daddy served each of us a slab of meat loaf, a mountain of mashed potatoes, and a pile of peas. Evan looked at me, questioning. I just shook my head with nothing to offer, good or bad.

Finally, Andy came breezing through the front door. He looked frazzled and grimaced as he set his book bag down by the front door.

"Hi, honey." Mom started fixing him a plate.

He took his coat off with another grimace but quickly recovered.

Mom filled him in on our antics, and I held my breath, hoping that he wouldn't mention anything about Evan's artwork.

"Do you know anything?" she asked.

Andy shook his head and swallowed his mouthful.

"I've been at the library the whole time. From about four o'clock until just now. At the library."

Mom nodded, satisfied with his answer, but Andy went on.

"I was working on a project this whole time. Until just now."

"Uh-huh. We've got it," Daddy said.

Andy's eyes darted around, and he was jolted when Mom asked him what the project was about.

"Huh? Oh . . . right. It's just a project for my government class." He reached for the basket of rolls, and we all noticed something that looked like a bandage under the sleeve of his shirt and a definite look of pain on his face.

"What's that?" Mom asked, reaching for his arm. Andy yelped and pushed her hand away.

"What's the matter with you? What happened, honey? Did you get hurt?"

"It's nothing. Really."

I think I actually saw tears in his eyes as he sorted through the basket of rolls.

"Obviously, it's something." Like a dog with a bone, she persisted and grabbed his sleeve. She pulled it up and revealed a square bandage on his upper arm. The skin around the bandage was red and irritated.

"Ugh!" Andy groaned. "Mom, don't touch it, please!"

"Honey, I'm worried. You've obviously been hurt."

And then, in a voice choked with pain, Andy confessed. "It's a tattoo."

His words hung in the air until Mom shattered the silence by ripping the bandage off. The sight of my six-foot-four-inch brother reduced to tears and cowering in his seat was something I never could have imagined.

"It's my basketball number. You know, since it's my senior year. The whole team did it."

"It washes off, right?" She pointed a finger at the wound. Andy yelped again in fear that she was going to touch it.

"No." His voice was a squeak.

Glassy-eyed with shock, Mom flopped back into her seat.

"What's next?" she asked no one in particular.

Evan started laughing uncontrollably, and relief washed over me, because this would definitely take the attention away from my own misdeeds.

"Evan, be quiet. Kathy, calm down," Daddy said.

"Oh, no, I will not! Don't even try to tell me 'boys will be boys' on this one!" She got up to take a closer look at Andy's oval tattoo. I could hardly make out the colors or the number *16* because it was so red and puffy.

"Does it hurt a lot?" Mom asked.

"Yeah," Andy admitted.

"Good," she said. Then she threw up her hands. "I just don't know anymore." She eyed each of us and stormed up to her room.

Daddy rubbed his face and massaged his temples. "Evan, I said quit laughing." He eyed Evan, but it was no use, so he turned his attention to Andy. "Did they tell you how to care for it?"

Andy nodded and worked at replacing the bandage.

"What's done is done. Your mom will get over it."

This comment stopped Evan's laughter cold.

"That's it? He lied about where he was all afternoon and he probably forged a consent form or showed some kind of fake ID to get his tattoo, and you say what's done is done?"

"I didn't forge anything!" Andy grimaced, and his bandage flopped onto the table.

"Then let's see your fake ID," Evan said.

"Shut up!" Andy yelled.

"Both of you, quit," Daddy said. "Evan, your brother has a good record with your mother and me. A history of trust goes a long way."

Andy smiled and looked at his arm.

"You, on the other hand—don't even get me started."

Evan blinked and sat back in his chair. He watched Daddy hold Andy's arm, gently inspecting the tattoo artist's work. I saw a look of pride and even a bit of envy in Dad's face as he quizzed Andy about the experience.

Evan got up from the table and went upstairs without so much as a glance from Dad. I started to get up from the table too, but Daddy stopped me.

"Hold on, there. You'll start by doing the dishes tonight. You're grounded until you explain yourself."

I wondered about my history of trust. But I was struck again by the fact that I was not upset. I knew that I was doing the right thing, and I felt stronger, older.

"So?" Daddy asked.

My only answer was to start clearing the dishes from the table.

"Hmm." I could feel him watching me as I got to work on the meatloaf mess. Then he and Andy got up and went to sit on the couch.

While I was up to my elbows in dishes, I figured Evan had slipped out to see the owls. Daddy and Andy were watching TV, and Mom was doing whatever she does when she's angry with one of us—and on this night, she was triple angry.

"Do you have homework?" Daddy asked when I was finished with the kitchen. I nodded. "Get it done," he said. I sat alone at the table and did what I could, though it was amazingly hard to concentrate on solving equations after the day I'd had. When I was finished, Daddy sent me to bed.

On my way to my room, I stopped by Evan's room. He was lying on his bed. I could smell the night air in his room and knew I'd guessed right.

"How were the owls?" I asked.

He stared at me for a moment, then whispered, "Beautiful."

Chapter 15

The next morning, Mom was at my bedroom door ready and waiting for an explanation.

"Your father told me you're grounded until you explain what you were up to."

I rubbed the sleep from my eyes and looked up at her. "I can't," I said, pulling my covers up to my chin for a last few seconds of warmth before I got up and faced the morning cold.

Mom put her hands on her hips, lips pressed together in a thin, angry line.

"Get up and get ready for school. I'll pick you up if it's raining when school gets out."

By the time I got downstairs for breakfast, Daddy had already left for work. Andy was trying to eat with his left hand, since his right arm was so sore.

"Can I see it?" I asked.

"No."

Evan and I shared amused grins.

"Do you think it's infected?" Mom asked.

"No," Andy said, taking one last bite of Froot Loops.

As he grabbed his backpack, Mom noticed that it had started to rain.

"Andrew, could you give Samantha a ride?"

"Yeah, but hurry up," he said to me. "I don't want to be late."

"Yeah, he needs time to compare tattoos with the other knuckleheads," Evan teased.

"Right. *I'm* the knucklehead."

"Don't start, boys," Mom said. She was still in her bathrobe and moved as if she were carrying ten-pound weights on her shoulders. Without the usual kiss good-bye, she walked upstairs to get dressed. I looked after her and caught myself hoping she'd at least wave good-bye. When her bedroom door closed with no wave, it felt worse than the slap last night.

"Let's go, Sam," Andy said.

I grabbed a granola bar for breakfast and said good-bye to Evan.

"Wait," he said to me and dashed upstairs. He came back down and pressed a key into my hand.

"Can you get my bike at the depot?" he whispered. I nodded and slung my backpack over my shoulder. I dashed out to where Andy was waiting in his car, engine running. In just minutes the rain had become a downpour, and I was glad for the ride, no matter how stinky his car was.

"Don't get granola crumbs all over my seat," Andy warned as he backed down the driveway. Was he kidding? There were old fries at my feet, and I'd had to pull a balled-up burger wrapper from my seat before I sat down. When he came to a quick stop at an intersection, an empty soda cup rolled into my feet. Then my oldest brother really caught me by surprise.

"I know what you and Evan were doing last night."

Jolted, I turned the radio on and tried to act like I hadn't heard him. He turned the radio off, took a second to recover from the painful reach. "I mean, I don't see what the big deal is, and I think it's cool that you're willing to take heat from Mom and Dad just so Evan can show off his artwork. He is really good at it."

"You promise you won't tell?"

"Promise. Go ahead and turn the radio back on."

I did.

"Turn it up," he said. So I cranked the dial and John Cougar Mellencamp sang something about a couple named Jack and Diane.

"Thanks, Andy," I said, looking up at my big brother.

As he pulled into the long line of cars easing up to the front of the elementary school, he acknowledged my thanks with a cool shrug.

"Crap, this is going to take forever." We inched along in the traffic jam of moms and dads dropping their kids off. "You can get out here and run, can't you?"

I looked out at the torrential rain. We were at least a half block away from the school driveway.

"Can't you?" he urged. So much for the love fest.

I gathered up my backpack and with a quick glare pushed the door open, climbed out, and splashed my way to the front of the school. Andy pulled out of line, made a U-turn, and sped away.

"I wish I had older brothers like you," Gilbert said as he met me at our classroom door.

"You want older brothers who make you run in the rain instead of dropping you off like your mom said to?" I asked, squatting down and wringing out my pant cuffs.

Gilbert picked up my backpack for me. He looked miserable.

"What's wrong, Gilbert?"

"My dad was supposed to take me for Thanksgiving, but he's going to his girlfriend's family's house."

"Can't he take you?"

Gilbert shrugged and shook his head. I gave up on getting any drier and stood up.

"The thing is, my mom booked a cruise for herself. It's one of those cruises for single people." He scrunched up his face at the thought.

"Jeez, Gilbert."

"I think my grandma's going to come stay with me."

This was not good. Grandma McNutt was the kind of grandma who made you wash your hands and face all the time and asked if you'd had a good BM that day. If not, she had a bottle of castor oil and a spoon in her purse.

He was quiet for a moment, and then his eyes lit up. "Hey, what were you doing last night? Your mom really freaked out and then my mom freaked out because she thought I was trying to cover for you."

"Oh, yeah." I started to explain when the bell rang. "I'll tell you later."

Gilbert handed me my backpack and we headed inside. Between being soaked and distracted by Gilbert's problems and the adventures from the night before, it was impossible to concentrate on fractions or pronouns. I was pretty sure I failed the test on Mesopotamia. And when Mrs. Teedle called on me to read aloud, I wasn't even on the right page. Gilbert bailed me out quickly, but not before Mrs. Teedle expressed her disappointment in my lack of concentration.

I started to read.

"Speak up," Mrs. Teedle snapped.

I started again.

"Louder, please."

I felt my face get hot and started one more time. Not really any louder, but Mrs. Teedle gave up on getting any more from me, and after a few sentences she called on someone else.

A while later a folded piece of paper landed on my desk. Huddled in my seat, I opened it carefully. It was a drawing of Mrs. Teedle with googly eyes and her tongue sticking out. The speech bubble above her head said, "My wig's too tight! Ahhh!"

I struggled to keep from laughing out loud and glanced at Gilbert, who was smiling. It was just what I needed. I folded the picture and slipped it into my pocket.

Somehow we survived the day. It wasn't raining after school, so Gilbert and I walked to the depot, where I was happy to find Evan's bike. Then we headed home, and along the way I filled him in on everything from the night before.

"See? Having older brothers is really cool. At least you have someone to go on adventures with."

I felt sorry for Gilbert. He shivered with the cold and looked smaller than usual.

"You want to spend Thanksgiving with your dad, right?"

"More than anything."

"Talk to him, then. I mean, really talk to him. Just the two of you."

"I don't know."

"You need to talk to your dad, because this isn't really about Thanksgiving." I looked at my best friend.

"Well, it's not about Valentine's Day!" he exclaimed, looking at me like I was crazy.

My shoulders fell, and I struggled to figure out what I was trying to say. "Okay. This is about Thanksgiving, but it's not. It's more than that. Thanksgiving is just one day."

"Right. And I don't want to spend it washing my hands, and you know what else."

"Call your dad," I said when we got to Gilbert's house.

"Maybe." He turned and jogged up the front steps, tripped on the last one, and sprawled out on his porch. Pressed under the weight of his backpack, he called, "I'm okay!"

I waved good-bye and walked on. The rest of the way home I checked the sky for rainbows. A wind had picked up, moving the white and gray mountains of clouds along. When enough were pushed together to block the sun, it was dark and cold. When the clouds parted, the sun was so bright the puddles sparkled and the leaves shimmered with clinging droplets of water. I shaded my eyes and scanned the sky. No rainbows.

Chapter 16

At home, Mom met me at the door. "Set your things inside. We have errands to run." She had her purse in one hand and an umbrella in the other. She was wearing a pink slicker and waterproof boots with matching pink trim.

"Come on," she urged. Then she leaned back inside. "Evan, let's go."

She marched out to the car. I tossed my backpack inside and saw Evan pull himself off the couch. He moved slowly. By the look on his face I could tell it had been a long day for him.

Our first stop was the craft store. The mission added two more tables, which meant two more centerpieces. From there we went on to check the boxes the Women's Guild had set out for the canned food drive. Mom was not happy to see that no box was more than a quarter full.

"Hmm. Well, I guess we do have until Monday," she said, moving on to B&B Pharmacy.

"What happens then?" I asked, catching the door she let close because she was so far ahead.

"We'll pick up everything and ship it off to the Family Help Organization. It'll go to families in need all over the county. At this rate, though, we won't help nearly as many families as last year."

I had to jog to keep up with her as we went back to the car. When Mom had errands to run, she was all business. "No lollygagging," she always said. Of course, Evan worked at moving slowly, and a few times, we even lost sight of him as we hustled along. This made Mom angry, and she snapped at him to get a move on. He threw up his hands and glowered.

"What's the hurry?" he asked.

"You know what the hurry is," she said as we got back into the car. All the way to our next stop, which was Glenda's house, Mom rattled off the things that had to be done between now and Thanksgiving. She was red-faced and sputtering by the time we got there, so she had to take a moment to freshen up before we went in. I caught a glimpse of a satisfied grin on Evan's face. Things were getting worse between Mom and Evan.

Glenda was the vice president of the Women's Guild, and the two women needed to finalize plans for the mission feast. I always liked Glenda's house. It was warm and smelled like she was baking a cake or a fresh batch of brownies. She and her husband had two huge dogs, mutts that claimed most of the furniture in the family room. Mom couldn't believe Glenda allowed the dogs to lounge on her furniture with their shaggy mix of brown, gray, black, and white fur.

Evan and I squeezed onto the couch between the two dogs, and they took turns licking our faces, which got us laughing. Mom snapped her fingers and pointed at the floor next to her, indicating that she wanted us to stand there and keep out of trouble. I pulled myself away from the dogs and noticed that I was covered in fur. Mom did not look happy. Evan stayed right where he was.

"Oh, my dogs just love kids!" Glenda laughed and made a halfhearted attempt at controlling them. "Bonnie! Clyde! Be good, now!" The two dogs stood up on the couch, made three awkward circles, and flopped down, proudly licking their chops and wagging their tails. Evan sat between the two, patting their heads and grinning at Mom. I knew she wanted to yank him off the couch, but she wasn't about to embarrass herself in front of Glenda.

Instead she got back to business and ran through a list from memory. Glenda said, "Check . . . Check . . ." to each item until Mom mentioned the reading of the Thanksgiving story.

"Well . . ." Glenda started.

Mom was struck with concern. "What?"

"We'd assigned it to Susan Parks, but she got a call from her aunt in Idaho. Her uncle is ailing, and it looks like she's going there for Thanksgiving."

"Oh," Mom said. And after a moment's thought, "How about Karla?"

"She left for Mammoth this morning."

"Linda?"

"She has to leave early. Isn't it obvious? You should read the story. You deserve the honor. You've literally put the whole event together."

Glenda looked positively overjoyed and, before Mom could say another word, dashed into the next room and came out with a book. She held it out to Mom, who swallowed nervously and, to my surprise, took my hand in hers, which was cold and clammy. With her other hand she took the book that had a picture of two Pilgrims offering a cornucopia to two solemn-looking Native Americans. I was pretty sure that wasn't how the story really happened.

"Can't you read it?" Mom's voice wavered, and Glenda looked confused. I looked at Evan, who was watching intently.

"I'm hosting Thanksgiving for my entire family at my house this year, remember?"

"Right." Mom nodded. "I knew that. Well, it's up to me, then. Allrighty, I guess that's it for now."

Glenda walked us to the door and had to close it quickly before Bonnie or Clyde went bounding out.

"Try to get some of that fur off before you get in the car."

I ran my hands over my shirt and slapped my pant legs, but all I managed to do was move it around. Evan did the same. Mom groaned.

"We don't have time for this. I've got two more centerpieces to make, and dinner to cook. Get in," she said, tossing the book into the backseat next to Evan.

I got into the car, but Mom didn't start it up right away. She just sat there, staring ahead.

"Mom?"

She didn't respond.

"Mom," I said again, and gently touched her

arm. She didn't acknowledge me but started the car and backed down the driveway.

At the first stop sign, she just sat there. Drivers to our left and right waved her on, but she didn't move, so they crossed in front of us, and then the car behind us honked.

"Huh?" Mom glanced in the rearview mirror.

"I think it's your turn," I said. I looked at Evan, who had scooted forward in his seat and had his arms wrapped around the headrest of my seat. He was looking at Mom curiously.

"Oh. Right." Mom drove on and tried to act like everything was normal. She giggled and winked at me, but her smile was phony and offered no reassurance. Then, to make things worse, she almost ran a red light.

"Mom!" Evan shouted, and she sucked in her breath as she skidded to a stop.

"What's the matter?" I asked, feeling a strange kind of panic growing.

"Nothing. I just have a lot on my mind." She started up slowly when the light turned green.

"I know. Maybe Mr. Gilroy can read the story. He runs the mission. Or better yet, maybe one of the guests can read the story. That would be nice."

"Mom," I said with growing uneasiness. "I think Glenda wants you to read it. You deserve to. Like she said, you've put so much work into making the day special for all those people."

To this she only shook her head. The sky grew dark with thick gray clouds and the rain started. We drove along with only the swish of the windshield wipers breaking the strange silence in the car. Then Evan said something that would change our lives forever.

"You can't read, can you." It was not a question.

I spun around in my seat, wondering who he was talking to. Mom made a strange noise and fumbled with the windshield wiper switch as the rain began to pour. The car swerved, and she struggled to keep control.

"You can't read!" Evan said it louder this time. I looked from him to Mom and back at him. Evan was wide-eyed, holding the book up so it filled the rearview mirror. Mom gripped the steering wheel.

"Don't be ridiculous," she said through clenched teeth.

"YOU CAN'T READ!" Evan screamed it this time.

"It's not true!" Mom cried. She started gasping for air, and her whole body was shaking. The car swerved again, and this time Mom did not regain control. She slammed on the brakes, but it wasn't enough. We sailed off the side of the road and into a large redwood tree. I was thrown forward, hitting my head on the vent in the dashboard.

The three of us sat in stunned silence for a moment. Rain beat on the roof of the car, and then lightning flashed, and I caught a glimpse of the front end of the car resting at an angle against the tree. Thunder roared, and I became aware of a sharp pain above my right eye. Something warm and wet ran down the side of my face.

"Oh, God! Oh, no!" Mom reached out to me with trembling hands. "Baby . . ." She touched the side of my face, and by the light of another flash of lightning, I saw blood on her fingers and started crying. She snapped into action and reached into her purse for a wad of Kleenex. She handed it to Evan, who leaned forward and gently pressed it against the cut on my head.

"Are you okay?" she asked Evan.

"Yeah," he said in a shocked whisper. Then Mom looked herself over and scanned the dashboard. She turned the keys in the ignition, and the car started up right away as if it had just been parked for a moment.

"Okay. Baby, we'll get you home in just a minute. Here we go."

Slowly she backed the car up onto the road.

"Home? Sam's really hurt. I think we should go to Emergency or something." Evan pulled the blood-soaked Kleenex away from my head and quickly replaced it.

"Ouch!" I cried.

"We're going home. I need your father's help. I need him . . ." She was gulping panicked breaths. Waves of dizziness surged through my body, and I thought I was going to throw up. I felt relief when our house came into sight, and I saw Daddy's car.

"Graham!" Mom started screaming as soon as the car was in "park." She ran inside, and in a second, Daddy came dashing out behind her. He didn't even have shoes on, and I saw his white socks turn brown in the mud.

He pulled the car door open, Mom hovering behind him. Evan didn't let go of the Kleenex as Daddy leaned down to get a look at me. Without a word he scooped me up and carried me to his car. Mom was right behind him.

"Get the door, Kathy!" he yelled. But Mom hesitated.

"Let's get her inside and see if she really needs a doctor."

Daddy made a kind of growling noise, and Evan

was right there pulling the door open so Daddy could set me in the front seat.

"Graham, people will know I got into an accident if . . ."

Dad gave her such a fierce look she did not finish her sentence. Evan got into the backseat, and Daddy strode around to his side of the car. I smelled his cologne, and with blurry eyes, I watched Mom get smaller and smaller as we backed down the driveway. She just stood there, crying in the pouring rain.

Chapter 17

"What happened?" Daddy asked as he sped to the hospital in Lafayette.

"She . . ." Evan struggled to speak. "Lost control." His voice was thick with tears.

"Samantha, honey, do you feel sick to your stomach?"

How did he know? The bleeding had slowed, but my head was pounding.

When we got to the hospital, I was glad Daddy carried me, because I don't think I could have walked. My legs felt weak, and I kept trying to concentrate on not throwing up.

I lost the battle while Daddy, Evan, and I waited in a small curtained cubicle. I was embarrassed as an orderly in green scrubs mopped up my mess and then gave me a pink peanut-shaped tub to hold in case I felt sick again.

Daddy held me on his lap and rubbed my back. I knew I was too old for that, but it made me feel better—safer. Evan sat in a chair beside us, staring at the floor, and I wondered what he was thinking. Every once in a while he would look at me, and then his eyes would dart away again. I'm sure he was just as glad that Daddy didn't ask more about what had happened. I guess it was enough to know that Mom had lost control of the car in the storm. He knew nothing of the storm that was going on inside the car when we crashed.

Once the doctor determined that I had a mild concussion, she announced that she would "get started on those stitches."

"No! I don't want stitches!" I screamed, and actually tried to get up from the table.

"Hold on there, Samantha. We need you to be a brave girl for us."

Before I knew it, they had me strapped to the table. The pain was unbelievable. One nurse's entire job was to hold my head still, and I wanted to clobber the doctor, who kept saying, "Just a little sting." I wondered what she would call a big sting.

Daddy and Evan held my hands. I couldn't see

them, but I heard Evan sniffling, and at one point a nurse asked him if he wanted to step out.

"No," he said, and stayed right where he was. Daddy tried to comfort me, but I couldn't concentrate on what he was saying.

When I didn't think I could stand anymore, I begged the doctor to stop. Evan's sniffling became louder.

"Please!" I cried.

"We're almost done," she said in a calm voice. "Almost . . ." She pulled, tied, clipped, pulled, tied, and clipped again. "Done," she said, and the nurse let go of my head. Daddy leaned over me, grimacing. Evan looked white as a sheet, his eyes red and teary.

"That took six stitches," the doctor said, pulling off her gloves and tossing them into a trash can she opened with her foot. "It should heal nicely, with minimal scarring. She'll be sore for a few days. Check on her throughout the night tonight about every hour or so." She turned to the nurse. "Give them an ice pack for the ride home." Then to Daddy again, "Jan here will get her bandaged up. Give your regular doctor a call for a follow-up." And then she dashed out through the curtain and into another cubicle. "Hi, there," she greeted her next victims.

"My little girl beat her brothers' records." Daddy

tried to sound lighthearted. "Evan's had three stitches, and I think Andy's only had five."

This was not a record I was happy about, although Jan must have thought it was funny, because she laughed as she taped a piece of gauze on my forehead. When she was finished, she undid the strap and helped me sit up. I felt dizzy, and I was happy to let Daddy carry me again. On the way out to the car, I realized that he still didn't have shoes on. Just dirty, wet socks.

I sat in the backseat with Evan. For most of the ride, I held the ice pack in my lap. It hurt too much to press it to my forehead. The rain had stopped, and there was a full moon. Mom met us at the door and became hysterical when she saw me and learned that I had gotten six stitches.

"Oh, honey! My baby girl!" she cried.

"I want to go to bed," I said. I had such a headache that the glare of the lights forced my eyes shut, and Mom's panicked voice was like a hammer tapping each word on my brain.

Daddy carried me upstairs, and Mom turned my bed down. She slipped off my shoes, and I was asleep before Daddy let go of me.

Chapter 18

At one point during the night, I woke to find Mom checking on me.

"Mom," I whispered.

"Yes?" She leaned down. I could see her face and that she was still dressed, though rumpled and untucked.

"What time is it?" That wasn't really what I wanted to ask.

"Three o'clock in the morning." She started for my door again.

"Mom?"

She stopped.

"Is it true?" She did not turn back to face me with an answer. "Sleep," she said, and left before I could ask again.

I did sleep until I became aware again of someone watching over me. This time it was Daddy, and it
was just about sunrise. The same spicy cologne from
the night before tickled my nostrils as he pulled my
covers up and tucked them around me. I saw his look
of concern as he gazed at my face.

"Daddy."

"Hush, baby," he said as he gently brushed my
hair from my forehead and kissed me on the nose.

"Is it true?" I asked, but he just looked at me,
confused.

"Is what true?" he asked, and my breath caught
in my throat.

I closed my eyes, too tired to say more.

The next time I woke, the sun was bright. I
opened my eyes, closed them, and then something
made me open them again.

"Perfect," I said to myself as a watercolor painting of a rainbow came into focus. I plucked it off of
my nightstand and realized that it was painted on the
inside of an envelope torn completely open.

Smiling to myself, I set it back on the nightstand.

I stood and then quickly sat again until the room
stopped spinning. Then I got up and walked down
the hall.

"Hey, squirt." Andy came out of his room and

leaned down to look at me. "Man, you got off a lot worse than the car. It doesn't even have a scratch."

"Terrific," I said, and went on to the bathroom.

Every move hurt, and just as I made it to the toilet, Mom's voice rang out, sending electric shocks up my spine to my pounding head.

"Honey, how are you?" I didn't answer. I think my head would have split open if I'd tried.

I finished, flushed, and pulled the door open. She was right there, asking again how I was. What could I say?

"I'll get you some aspirin." She left me standing in the hall.

In a moment she was back with a cup of water and two white tablets.

"Better?" she asked.

"Not yet."

"Come downstairs. I'm making your favorite." She put an arm around me, and we walked down to the kitchen.

Daddy came in from the garage, carrying Evan's door.

"Look who's up!" He smiled, leaned the door against the cupboards, and gave me a quick squeeze. Then he held my chin and scrutinized my face.

"Still beautiful," he declared, and let go with another kiss on the nose.

"Here you go." Mom set a steaming bowl of oatmeal with brown sugar and butter in front of me. She didn't know that my real favorite breakfast was blue chocolate-chip pancakes with chocolate syrup.

I looked over at Evan, who was standing by his door holding a hammer and the pins for the hinges. I gave him my best "What the hell is going on?" look. He shrugged and followed Daddy upstairs.

Each pound of the hammer made my head throb, and I was grateful that it didn't take much to replace the door. When he was done, Daddy went out to the garage to put the finishing touches on three birdhouses some secretaries at work were going to buy. I watched Mom rinse the breakfast dishes as Andy finished his cup of coffee. Since he was going to college next year, he decided it was time to start drinking coffee. Although I think it was more cream and sugar than anything.

"Bye." He handed Mom his cup to rinse, picked up his gym bag, and dashed out the door. I guess his tattoo was on the mend.

As I ate my oatmeal, I could feel the aspirin beginning to work. Mom bustled about like it was any normal Saturday morning. She did a little dusting and a little laundry and even hummed as she worked.

"What?" she asked when she was passing through the kitchen and caught my stare. Did she really not know what I was thinking about?

"Does your head still hurt?" she asked.

"Yeah, but that's not what's bothering me."

"You should go lie down. In a little while I need to take the centerpieces to the mission and check on the supplies for Thursday. Daddy and Evan will be home all day."

"Mom." I got up and followed her to the laundry room.

"Go lie down." She pulled laundry from the dryer and started folding towels and T-shirts. She was so rattled that the things she folded ended up in a balled mess.

"Mom," I started again. "Is it true?" My words bounced against the cold tile of the laundry-room floor.

"Samantha, please." She kept her back to me.

I went to the garage, where Daddy was working. The scent of wood shavings was strong, and I could see little yellow curls of wood billowing out of a hole he was making in one of the houses.

"Honey, you shouldn't be out here in bare feet,"

he said when he finally noticed me and stopped drilling.

"Did Mom tell you what happened?"

He nodded, pulled his safety glasses back over his eyes, and picked up his drill.

"I mean what *really* happened?"

He pulled the glasses off and looked at me. "I know it was scary last night. I'm just so glad you weren't hurt worse." He put his drill down and pulled me into a hug. Less than satisfied, I went to Evan's room.

"What's going on?" I didn't speak in more than a whisper, because my head was starting to throb again. I gestured at his door, and he just grinned.

"It's typical," he said.

I sat on his bed and watched him prepare to make another watercolor painting. "It's true, huh?"

He looked at me for a moment. "That Mom can't read? You bet. Have you ever seen her pick up a book or a newspaper? She didn't exactly read us *Green Eggs and Ham* when we were little." He had a point, but something deep inside still wanted to hope that maybe this was all some kind of wild misunderstanding.

"She reads magazines when we go to the doctor's office or the dentist."

"Those have pictures!" he yelled, and I winced. "Why do you think I got my door back?" It was one of those questions I wasn't supposed to answer, because he already had the answer, and he was going to tell me no matter what. "It's a lot easier to put a door back than to actually admit the truth." There it was, and he was right. He went on, despite the fact that I was cradling my head as if I could keep a headache from coming on again.

"I've been watching her for a while. She does things like I do. It's amazing how you can find ways to get around actually having to read. She memorizes things people tell her, and you've tasted the fact that she never uses a cookbook. Who signs all the notes from school? Huh? Who helps with homework unless it's adding or subtracting?"

I needed to lie down, but I didn't want to be alone, so I eased myself onto his bed. Evan turned on his radio and started another painting.

"Did they even talk about what happened last night?" I asked after a moment.

"Some. Dad got pretty mad at Mom about how she didn't want anyone to know she'd been in an accident, but they dropped it. It makes sense that Mom wouldn't want anyone to know about it. She's perfect. And all I know is I woke up this morning and Mom was all excited about putting my door back on."

"This is crazy," I said. "How can she . . ." My head began to throb again. Evan focused on his work.

"Do you think Daddy knows?" I asked with a surge of nausea, and this wasn't from my injury. It was the kind of nausea you get when you realize things aren't what you thought they were.

Evan nodded and made the first strokes with his brush, the brown branches of a tree. "Incredible," he said, not taking his eyes off of his work, "what people are able to ignore."

I curled up on his bed, comforted by the music and the sight of him working on his art.

The next time I woke, I was startled to see that the sun had set. I was alone in Evan's room, and at some point he must have pulled a blanket over me. I realized that I hadn't seen my cut and wondered what it looked like, so I eased myself off of Evan's bed and made my way to the bathroom. My right eye was black and blue. Slowly, I pulled the bandage off, and my stomach turned at the sight of a scabbed line of six little black knots that ran along my eyebrow.

"We can put some makeup on your eye so it's not that noticeable on Monday."

I was so focused on my eye that I hadn't noticed Mom and practically jumped out of my skin. Without turning to look at her, I asked again, "Is it true?"

"Samantha." She sighed and paused for a long moment. Then she grabbed my shoulders and turned me to face her. "I have raised three children. I am a successful committeewoman. I make a difference in our community." I heard what she was saying, but she had tears in her eyes, and she would not look right at me. The question of whether she actually graduated from high school burned in my brain, but I couldn't ask it.

No amount of makeup could hide the bruising, and I caused quite a stir when I got to school on Monday. Mom had called that morning to explain, and when Mrs. Teedle saw me, she told me how sorry she was, and that she was glad I was okay, and if I needed anything, to just ask. Gilbert was shocked, and I promised to tell him everything after school.

We went straight to his tree house. I figured that I wasn't grounded anymore and wanted to delay going home as long as possible. Gilbert was riveted by my every word, and I held nothing back.

"But your mom's a grown-up."

"So?"

"So, she has to be able to read. Grown-ups can read."

"All I know is things are horrible in my house," I said, running my finger along the notches Gilbert had made when he was counting his jawbreaker licks.

"Guess what I'm going to do?" he said, looking at me through the wrong end of his binoculars.

"What?"

"I'm going to stay up here in this tree house until my dad says I can come to Thanksgiving with him and his girlfriend."

"Really?"

He pulled his binoculars away from his face and nodded with a determination I had never seen before.

"Wow." I was impressed. I didn't mention that his mom could just get a regular ladder and climb up and get him. At least he was taking a stand. "This is what I was talking about the other day!" I cried happily.

"Not that again."

"Gilbert! Samantha! It's getting late. Dinner will be ready soon, Gil!" his mom called, and for a brief second, I saw my best friend waiver.

"Here we go," I said with a rush of nervous butterflies. "Stay strong." I threw the rope ladder down, and as soon as my feet hit the ground, Gilbert reeled it back up and waved good-bye.

"Where's Gilbert?" his mom asked as I made my way to the front door. Somehow I had hoped she wouldn't ask me that.

"Still up there. Bye." I rushed out the front door, not giving her a chance to quiz me further.

Gilbert wasn't at school the next day, and when the bell rang I ran the entire way to his house. When I got there I saw his Dad's VW van parked in the driveway. This had to be a good sign. As I walked past his house, I caught a glimpse of Gilbert and his father up in his tree house. Gilbert was talking, and I could see a smile on his face. He must have been excited, because he was using his hands a lot and his Dad was nodding.

At home, Andy was practicing free throws, and I could see that our parents weren't home.

"Hey, squirt. Want to go to Nation Burger? My treat."

"Sure."

"Go get Evan," he said, aiming and firing another perfect basket.

Chapter 19

At Nation Burger we enjoyed games of Pac-Man and tried out the newest game, Frogger. Evan said he preferred Pac-Man, and so did I. Andy even took a turn. I gave Mike, formerly known as Pimple, my nicest smile. He didn't seem to notice or appreciate it as much as I'd hoped, but that was okay.

When our food arrived, Andy was in the middle of making a ketchup pool for our fries when I finally asked him.

"Do you think Mom can't read?"

My question hung in the air, mingling with the smell of burgers grilling and the sounds of conversation. Evan sighed angrily and got up from the table. Andy stopped making a ketchup pool but still held the bottle over the tray.

"What does it matter? She's a good mom."

"It matters a lot," I said, suddenly not hungry. I looked to where Evan had dropped another quarter in the Pac-Man game.

"Sam, Mom had a hard time in school. She doesn't like to talk about it. So don't go bringing things up that don't need to be talked about. And no, I don't think she can't read. I just think things are hard for her sometimes. Look at all she does. Someone who can't read wouldn't be able to do what she does." He eyed me for a moment and went back to making what was more like a ketchup lake.

"I think you're wrong," I said. "And I think Mom is a liar."

Andy set the ketchup bottle down so hard, a little bit popped out from the top. He leaned toward me and spoke through clenched teeth. "You watch your mouth." But that was all he said, and then he saw a couple of friends come through the door and took his tray over to eat with them. I hadn't realized Evan was right behind me until he flopped down in his seat.

He looked over to where Andy sat smiling and sharing his fries with his friends. "Forget it, Sam. It doesn't matter to him, because he can read. He can do everything." Evan avoided my eyes and told me to eat as he gobbled three fries at a time.

The next day Gilbert was all smiles. As we sat on the parallel bars at recess, he told me about how his mom was hysterical at first, and that when she threatened to get the ladder, he thought it was all over.

"Then she said that my dad should see how pathetic this was, and she called him." Gilbert hopped off the bars. He was so excited, he had to stand to tell me the rest. "Of course he wasn't home. So she went back to begging me to come down, but I wouldn't. She told me I'd get a cold and that dinner was ruined and that this was all my dad's fault.

She kept calling my dad's house and leaving him all kinds of mean messages about how he was the worst father in the world. Then she'd come back out and yell at me. She said I'd be grounded if I didn't come down. Then she felt bad and said she'd get me a toy if I did come down. It was crazy." He stopped, out of breath.

"So? What happened next?"

"She just kept calling and calling, but he didn't call back. I was getting cold and I was starving, but I didn't care." He settled back onto the parallel bars. "I stayed up there the whole night, and I didn't even get an asthma attack. My dad must have been at his girl-friend's house, and of course, my mom doesn't have that number. Finally he called the next morning. I've never heard my mom yell like she did. He came over real fast, and I let him come up to my tree house. He brought a box of doughnuts, and we spent the whole day just talking."

"And?"

"And, my dad and I are going to have Thanksgiving together, just the two of us." He smiled triumphantly.

"See? You stood up for yourself, and it worked!"

Instantly, I was jolted by my own words. It was what Mrs. Brewster had said about taking a stand. I was starting to see things that had been right there for a long time, and it frightened me.

On Thanksgiving morning, I enjoyed as much of the Macy's Thanksgiving Day Parade as I could before Andy turned the TV to football. I hated football, so I looked for Evan and found him hard at work on his latest painting. It was the tree he'd started a few days ago. He'd filled it in with shades of green, and it was backed by a blue watercolor sky.

"Do you want to come to the art festival tomorrow?" he asked.

"Of course."

We shared smiles, and then Mom announced that we needed to get ready to go.

On the way out, I dashed over to Mom's car, wondering if the Thanksgiving book was still in the backseat. Sure enough, it was, and in a rush I opened the door and grabbed it. I believed Evan, but I still hoped that Mom would prove him wrong.

"Samantha, what are you doing? We're going in Daddy's car," Mom said.

"You forgot this." I ran over to her, holding up the book.

"I don't know that there will time for that today," Mom said quickly, but I was determined.

"Just in case," I said, holding the book out, leaving her no choice but to take it.

The mission was a busy place. We could smell the turkey before we even stepped inside. The kitchen crew was cooking huge pots of mashed potatoes and stirring a vat of gravy, and volunteers were setting dishes of cranberry sauce on the tables. The centerpieces Mom made looked really nice, and as I had figured, there were large orange candles set in the middle of each one. The hall where the meal was to be served was also used as a gym, and I noticed that there were basketball hoops folded up against the walls at each end.

The first task Evan and I were given was to set out the plastic forks, knives, and spoons. Andy folded napkins and set them at each place while Daddy helped carry the huge warming dishes out to a long row of tables at one end of the hall. At the other end of the hall, there was a stage set up. That was where speeches and thank yous would be made. That was where Mom would read the Thanksgiving story.

"We'll be serving buffet style," Mom said as she strung a "Welcome" sign across the entrance to the hall.

I lost track of the book. As the time for the meal approached, I became increasingly nervous and distracted. At one point I realized that I was setting plasticware at a table that was already set. Mom buzzed about, greeting different people and posing for pictures. Daddy looked on with such pride, and he told anyone he spoke to that this whole event was her doing.

"She's an incredible woman," he said over and over. I noticed that Evan was watching her too.

Finally, the head of the mission opened the doors, and the people filed in. Along with the kitchen crew, Evan, Andy, Daddy, and I replenished the serving dishes. I overheard many of the people say that this Thanksgiving was much better than last year's, and I knew this was because Mom had been in charge of it.

Toward the end of the meal, Mom took the stage, and I held my breath. Pumpkin pie was being served, and the whoosh of the canned whipped cream sounded throughout the hall. Mom had not taken even a moment to sit or have a bite of food. A couple of times Daddy offered to make her a plate, but she said she was too busy and excited to eat. She was thrilled because the event was a complete success.

Evan, Daddy, Andy, and I were seated at a table near the kitchen, and I had to prop myself up on my knees to see Mom. She started by thanking the kitchen crew and her fellow Women's League members, who had helped in organizing the traditional Thanksgiving feast. Where was the book? I felt my throat tighten, but I still made myself believe that in just a moment, she would step to the side of the stage and pick it up. Mom informed everyone that this year they were able to feed one hundred sixty people a traditional Thanksgiving meal, and that if she had her way, next year we would share Thanksgiving with over two hundred guests.

Every muscle in my body strained as she went on

to thank the people who ran the mission and to list all of the services the mission offered to the community. I noticed that she did all of this from memory and looked at Evan, who raised his eyebrows and nodded at me. Get the book, I thought. My heart started to pound. Next, Mom thanked the stores and organizations that had donated the food for the meal.

"And, last but not least, I would like to thank my family for helping today. I love you all so much." She blew us kisses, and my heart sank as I watched her return the microphone to the stand and step down from the stage. She went on to shake hands with people and pose for more pictures as she made her way through the crowd. I burst into tears.

Daddy dropped his fork. "What's the matter?"

What could I say?

"Samantha?" Daddy reached out to me. "Is something hurting you?"

I shook my head, but he ignored this and stood over me, trying to examine my eye. He held my head in his hands and turned it this way and that, trying to get a good look, which was impossible by candlelight.

"That's not it!" I cried, and pulled my head from his grasp. In the process, I lost my balance and tipped over in my chair with a loud crash. There was a startled hush in the conversation for a moment as Daddy helped me up. This made Andy laugh, which made me cry harder, and Mom rushed over.

"What's the matter?" she asked.

With tears streaming down my face, I looked at her. "You didn't . . ."

"Samantha," Mom said in a surprisingly harsh voice. "You need to stop crying. There's nothing to cry about." She patted my back and looked around at people, smiling and telling them everything was fine. "Just a little emotional today," she said in a voice straining to sound lighthearted.

"Go on out to the car if you can't stop crying," she whispered in my ear. "Evan, go with her."

She led me to the door with Evan right behind. The two of us went out to the car, and as soon as we were in the backseat, I let loose with a new round of sobs.

"She didn't read it!" I cried. Evan didn't say a word and offered me no comfort. He had been right, and it had to hurt him most of all.

By the time Mom, Dad, and Andy got to the car, I'd stopped crying.

"What's wrong with you?" Andy asked.

"Don't," Mom said. But Andy was not going to give up that easily.

"I'm serious. Mom worked hard to make this day nice for everyone, and you pitched a fit."

"Shut up!" Evan yelled.

"All of you be quiet, right now!" Daddy tried to put an end to it.

"No. I think you owe Mom an apology," Andy persisted as Daddy pulled onto the road.

I just buried my face in my hands.

"It's ridiculous. You're such a brat sometimes."

I think that if I hadn't been sitting between my two brothers, they would have come to blows. As it was, Evan reached across and gripped Andy's arm right on his tattoo. Andy made a strange kind of squealing noise and grabbed a handful of Evan's hair with his other arm. The two were locked in an angry grip, and I was pinned between them, trying to shield my eye from getting bumped.

"Good lord! Boys, stop! Stop right now!" Mom screamed.

"Don't make me pull this car over!" Daddy boomed, and then there was silence. It had been years since any of us had heard that threat, and the image of Daddy actually pulling the car over to discipline his nearly grown sons was so ridiculous that the two of them burst out laughing. They let go of each other, and I pulled my hands away from my face.

They were laughing so hard it got Mom started, and soon even Daddy had to crack a smile.

It was one of those times when things are so bad that laughing feels like heaven. Nothing was fixed, but we laughed harder than we had laughed in a long time.

When we got home, Mom went straight to her room. Andy and Daddy decided to go for a run.

"Let's hope you're in a better mood when we get home, young lady," Daddy said to me on his way. I watched the door close and settled in front of the TV. I discovered that I could watch *It's a Wonderful Life* in color on one channel and in traditional black and white on another. Evan joined me, and we flipped between the options, spending the most time on the black-and-white version. I liked the color, but Evan said it was too fake-looking.

Every once in a while, I looked up at Mom's room and wondered what she was thinking about. When Daddy and Andy got back from their run, they were sweaty and out of breath but smiling. They brought cold air heavy with the smell of fireplaces in with them, and the four of us sat down to our second helping of pumpkin pie from one of the leftover pies we'd brought home.

Dad didn't ask me how I was feeling. We passed the whipped cream around until nothing but air came out, and just like the laughter in the car, the donated pumpkin pie we shared that night was the best I had ever eaten. I guess when things are about as bad as they can get, something simple like second helpings of dessert can be sweeter than usual.

Chapter 20

The next morning Daddy declared a day of rest for Mom. He brought her breakfast in bed and told us kids to leave her be. Evan and I were just as glad for this, because it would make sneaking out to the Lafayette Art Festival a lot easier. The festival opened at one o'clock that afternoon.

Unfortunately, this allowed enough time for Evan to get roped into helping Daddy and Andy put the lights up on the house. I got to watch from the tire swing, and it was quite a production. The three of them carried clumps of lights out to the lawn and argued about how to untangle them. "This way! No! This way! You just made it worse!" I was glad no one suggested that I pitch in.

Last year Dad worked the whole day after

Thanksgiving putting up the lights on the house, and when he was finished he discovered that most of them didn't work. I'd never seen him so furious. It took a lot of pleading from Mom to convince him to replace the strings that didn't work. He spent the rest of the weekend getting the bad lights down and putting the replacements up.

"Don't pull a bulb loose. The whole string won't work if you do," Daddy warned. An hour later the strings were stretched out on the lawn in straight lines. Daddy plugged each string into the extension cord, and when he was sure they were all working, he propped the ladder against the roof and hooked the staple gun into his belt loop. Andy swore that he could not get up on the ladder because if he fell and broke something it would ruin his chances at a scholarship.

"Give me a break," Evan sneered.

"Don't start," Daddy said. "He's right."

"You always think he's right."

"I don't want to do this with you two fighting. If you can't control yourself, go to your room."

Evan was delighted.

"Punk," Andy muttered under his breath. Daddy started up the ladder and made his way across the roofline, while Andy fed the string of lights up to him. Each time a staple shot into the wood, I was startled and blinked at the noise. I found myself holding my breath, afraid that Daddy would fall or that he would staple through the wire, and it would be another weekend of angry decorating.

Then I caught a glimpse of something moving at the side of the garage. It was Evan, and I knew it was time to get going. Carefully I slipped away, and the two of us ran down the driveway. We ran until we were a safe distance and slowed to a stroll. Evan had bus money for us, and we enjoyed the sunny walk to the Orinda Depot.

There was an excited crowd at the festival. We joined a line of people at the door, and I noticed that some were dressed in their Sunday best, while others were more casual. But all were there to admire the work of artists like Evan. The man who had greeted us the night we turned in Evan's work announced that the judging for the amateur entries had already been done, and ribbons were posted next to the winning pieces. Judging for the professional entries would be done on Saturday. I felt a rush of butterflies and looked at Evan, who was breathing deeply, trying to remain calm.

Finally the doors opened, and some kind of classical music was playing as we slowly moved into the community center. A volunteer about Evan's age handed us brochures. Evan immediately tucked his into his back pocket, but I scanned the list until I found his name.

"Here you are!" I shouted. I held the brochure up with my finger under his name, but Evan only glanced briefly. He was desperately trying to find his sketch and quickly became frustrated. We couldn't see more than the floral prints of ladies' dresses and pinstripes of men's blazers as we were pressed in the middle of the crowd. Finally, in desperation, Evan took my hand and pulled me along toward one of the walls.

"Excuse me," I said over and over, avoiding the looks of irritation from the people we bumped into. I practically knocked one lady over, and she was about to give me a piece of her mind when Evan changed directions. We ducked through the sea of people and finally made it to an area that was less crowded.

"Where is it?" Evan said, his voice trembling. He looked left and right and stood on his toes trying to see across the room. Eventually people sorted themselves into smaller groups, and it was easier to move around. We walked past sketches of mountains, houses, people, and cats. We found the work that earned Third Place. It was a sketch of an old farmhouse with a broken-down wagon rotting to the side of it. In the distance a modern-day city loomed.

"Interesting. Very interesting," a man in a white blazer said as he gazed at the work. He put his horn-rimmed glasses on and then lifted them, squinting his eyes before he replaced his glasses and declared again, "Interesting."

Evan and I tried to keep from laughing.

First Place went to a drawing of the Eiffel Tower on a rainy day. Tourists with umbrellas stood in clumps beneath the tower, and a man holding a news-paper over his head dashed across a busy street.

"Such detail," the lady I'd nearly knocked over commented, and we moved on quickly.

We found the entry that earned Grand Prize, a painting of a bowl of fruit. *Flight* was a lot better than a bowl of fruit. I could draw a bowl of fruit.

"Look at this one." The woman waved her hus-band over and pointed. We followed, and there was *Flight*. Evan stood there frozen.

"It's beautiful. So lifelike," the woman said.

"Stunning," the man chimed in, moving closer for a better look. I pulled Evan forward, unable to resist the opportunity.

"My brother drew that." The couple turned to look at me.

"That one. My brother drew it. This is my brother." I had to tug to get him to move closer.

The woman smiled. "Congratulations," she said, shaking Evan's hand.

"Well done, son," the man said, clapping Evan on the back. Then the two moved on, and Evan and I were left standing in front of his entry in the Lafayette Art Festival. To the left of his framed sketch, there was a red ribbon. In the center, in gold lettering, it said, "Second Place."

Evan reached out and touched the ribbon. Then he stepped back from his work and nodded to himself. He looked so calm, so still.

"Second Place," he whispered.

A lady in a black dress with a white apron came by with a tray of clear plastic cups of sparkling cider. Evan and I each took a cup, and then another lady in the same kind of outfit offered us a tray of tiny pink, blue, yellow, and white cakes. We looked over the selection, and the lady explained that the cakes were called petit fours. We took two each. She smiled at us and quickly moved on before we took thirds.

Another man stepped forward to look at *Flight*.

"He drew it," I said, quickly pointing to Evan.

"Excellent," the man said. "Mind if I take a picture and ask you a few questions?" He had a huge camera slung over his shoulder, flipped open a yellow notebook, pulled a pencil from behind his ear, and looked at Evan.

"Ev." I nudged him. "He wants to interview you."

Evan snapped out of his happy trance and finally noticed the man.

"Can I ask you a few questions? Take a picture? I'm a reporter for the *Lafayette Gazette*," the man said.

"Sure." Evan flashed a quick grin at me and then gave the man his best serious-artist look.

"So, how long have you been an artist?"

"Since I can remember. I've always loved drawing."

"Do you do any other type of art? Painting? Sculpting?"

"I'm giving watercolors a try."

"He made me a watercolor rainbow," I added. The man looked up at me from his yellow notepad and smiled.

"How long did it take you to make this sketch?"

Evan gave this some thought. "I'm not sure. I like to work on one sketch for a while. Then I set it aside and work on other sketches. When it feels right, I go back."

"He has a whole closet full of sketches," I chimed

in again, and again the man smiled up at me from his yellow notepad, but he did not write down what I had to say. "You should see them," I added.

"Perhaps at another festival," the reporter said, and Evan's smile broke through his serious look. The reporter jotted a few more notes and then said, "So, your parents must be very proud." He waved his pencil at the milling crowd, figuring our parents had to be somewhere among the admirers.

"Not really," Evan said. The man started to write, and then Evan's words sank in.

"No?"

Evan did not repeat himself. Instead he just looked straight into the reporter's eyes. I wondered what he would think of the fact that a little more than a week ago, our mother actually threw Evan's artwork into the trash.

"Hmm. Well. How about school? Your art teachers must be impressed with your talent."

Evan snickered and couldn't come up with more of an answer than the shake of his head and a shrug.

"He doesn't have art teachers," I explained.

I couldn't imagine what the reporter was writing, but Evan and I watched him work for a few minutes, and then he looked up from his notes with a renewed smile.

"Okay, I just need a picture of you standing next to your award-winning sketch."

Evan handed me his empty cup and a balled-up napkin. I stood beside the reporter as he directed Evan to stand up straight, look into the camera, and smile. He snapped about five shots and then shook Evan's hand.

"If all goes well, you'll find my article in Sunday's edition of the *Lafayette Gazette*." And with that, the reporter dashed off to find his next subject. He had no idea that even if it made the paper, Evan would not be able to read the story.

"Let's go," Evan said.

"Wait. Don't you want to see what other people think about your sketch?"

"Second Place pretty much says it all," Evan replied. The mention of our parents must have really gotten to him. We both knew that no prize would matter when we got home that day or any day.

Evan took my hand, but I didn't move.

"Come on."

"Not yet."

"Sam, I don't exactly want to get stranded here again."

I folded my arms and refused to move. Then I swallowed hard. "This is a really special day for you, but it's just one little moment in time, and when it's over, you'll just go back to the way things are. Like when we sneak out to see the owls. They're beautiful moments, but then they're gone."

Evan looked at me like I was crazy. "What exactly was in your cider?" He teased and flashed a crooked smile at me.

"You're afraid to do something about not being able to read." The words just came out louder than the classical music and the art talk. Evan's smile vanished, but I continued. "Maybe Mom won't sign whatever forms it takes to get you tested, but if you asked for help, if you said to any one of your teachers that you wanted their help, needed their help, I know they'd do something." I was trembling, and it was as if we were the only people in the room.

"Why are you saying this?"

"Wouldn't it be nice if you didn't have to keep this a secret?" I asked, nodding toward *Flight.*

"Mom's the queen of secrets." Evan narrowed his eyes at me, and I saw his teeth clench. I knew he didn't like what I was saying, and I was sorry that it was coming out at one of the happiest times in his life, but I couldn't help it. I couldn't hold it in any longer.

"Talk to Dad." I reached out to him, but he flinched.

"I don't believe you," he said in the saddest voice I'd ever heard, and then he turned and walked away. I lost sight of him quickly in the crowd and realized that I'd better catch up, since he was the one with the bus money.

He was already at the bus shelter by the time I got to the entrance of the community center. And like clockwork, the bus came along just as I was about to cross the street. I dashed across and ran up to the bus, where the driver had already closed the door and was about to pull away.

"Hey!" I screamed and waved.

The driver looked surprised and opened the door.

"Hurry up," he said, and when I got to the top of the steps, I was stuck, no money and an impatient driver. I gulped and looked at Evan, who was at the very back of the bus. I was beginning to think that I was going to have to call Mom or Dad.

"Do you have money or not?"

I looked back at Evan, who had his arms folded and was staring out the side window, pretending not to notice me.

"Look, I've got a schedule to keep. Pay or get off."

With a lump in my throat, I stepped back and started to get off when I heard Evan. "Hold on. I've got it."

My lump vanished, and I thought all was forgiven as Evan dropped twenty-five cents into the slot. The machine swallowed the money, and the driver handed me a little brown ticket dated 11/26 and stamped "One way."

"Thanks," I said to Evan, and started to follow him. With a shove, he knocked me into one of the middle-row seats and continued on to the back alone.

I got the message and stayed put. Other passengers got on and off as we wound our way back to the Orinda depot, and when we got to our stop, I was hoping that Evan had cooled off but treaded lightly just in case.

It was sunny and warm as we walked along in silence. I was kicking myself for blabbing at the wrong time. But I really believed in what I had said and could not apologize. I even tried once, but it just wouldn't come out. Instead, the words "I'm not sorry" slipped out.

"So?" Evan said, picking up his pace.

"What I'm saying makes sense. You can get help."

"Shut up," he said, and then he whipped around

and stared at me with angry eyes. "What you're saying means that you think it's my fault that I can't read."

"No." I shook my head. "That's not it at all. It's not about fault."

He walked away from me, and I had to jog to keep up. When I lagged behind, he didn't look at me, but he slowed his pace a bit.

We took the long way home past Hank's Apple Orchard. Most of the trees were bare, and a rusty sign posted at one of the gates read "Closed for the Season" in big green letters. In silence we gazed through the chain-link fence at row after row of trees. On a few of the trees, missed apples, looking more like prunes, still hung from the branches.

As we came to the end of the orchard, there was one tree that rested against the fence. A few of its branches were within Evan's reach, and on one branch there were two perfect apples. Evan reached up, twisted, and pulled the fruit until it snapped and came loose in his hands. A couple of dead leaves fluttered to the ground. He rubbed the apples on his shirtfront and handed one to me. It was warm from the day of sunshine and tasted juicy and sweet.

"A bowl of fruit doesn't deserve Grand Prize," I said after a while. "It's not very original. My teacher made us draw a bowl of fruit when I was in fourth grade. Or maybe it was a cornucopia. I can't remember."

We approached the house, and Evan sneaked around back unnoticed.

"Where have you been?" Daddy asked when he saw me.

"Playing," I said. He was admiring his work, though the lights looked dim in the sunlight. He noticed a place where one string was drooping and moved the ladder over so he could climb up and add a staple for support.

Just then a car with a lighted Pizza Hut sign clamped in the passenger side window pulled up, radio blaring.

"There's dinner," Daddy said. He got down from the ladder, brushed his hands off, and told the delivery boy he'd be right back. I hadn't realized how late it was. On his way out to pay for the pizza, Daddy told me to set the table.

The five of us sat down to a dinner of pizza with the works, and I was glad I wasn't stuck with press-on nails this time as I devoured my pizza. I watched Mom eat, and from time to time she glanced at Daddy and thanked him for taking care of things so she could have the day to rest. And just like that it came out. I was saying the words before I even realized I was talking out loud.

"That time you picked us up in Lafayette, we were entering one of Evan's drawings in the annual art contest. But you—" I looked at Mom, "you didn't know that because you couldn't read the huge banner that said about the festival. You can't read, and neither can Evan. And you—" I looked at Daddy, "you can't keep doing nothing about it."

My family sat in stunned silence. I was shaking so hard I had to hold on to the table.

"Evan got Second Place, and you should be proud of that. He was even interviewed by a newspaper reporter, and when he asked Evan if his parents were proud of him, do you know what he said? 'Not really.' And the reporter was so confused."

"Samantha," Daddy tried, but I was unstoppable.

"You should never have thrown his artwork away. Even Andy knew better." I looked at him. His eyes were on his plate, and I continued. "Andy rescued Evan's drawings from the trash, and I found them, and Evan won. You should have heard people talking about how talented he is. They were amazed, and you should be, too."

I waited to see what was going to happen. At

least no one had stormed off. No one burst into tears. No one yelled. They were listening. They had heard me, just like Gilbert's parents heard him. Just like Mrs. Brewster said they would.

Mom was the first one to make a move. She got up and walked over to me. For a brief moment, I was frightened when she reached out to me, but her touch was gentle. She cradled my face, kissed my forehead, and went upstairs. Andy left the table next, and I listened to the sound of his car fade away. Daddy gathered the paper plates and napkins and threw them away. He wrapped the leftover pizza in foil and went out to the garage.

Evan and I were left sitting at the table. He nodded, then he, too, got up and went to his room. I sat at the table alone for a long time. I wasn't sure what exactly I had accomplished, but there was no going back now. Daddy came in from the garage and searched the junk drawer until he found what he was looking for. I followed him back out and watched him squeeze a thin line of glue onto one of his birdhouses.

"Can you hold this in place?" he asked me. I reached out, and he pressed my fingers against a domino-shaped piece of wood, a tiny shutter on the house.

"The festival runs until Sunday. If you and Mom wanted to go see Evan's drawing, you could. There's a big red ribbon next to it. One of the frilly kinds with 'Second Place' written in gold lettering."

Daddy was quiet for a long time, and then he laid a hand on mine, the one that was still pressing the shutter in place.

"I'd like that. We'll go."